The Pitch
Book I:
The Rubicon
Chronicles

AJ Todd

For The Goat

CONTENTS

ACKNOWLEDGMENTS

The Pitch: Book I of The Rubicon Chronicles has been a labor of pure love, and it would not exist if not for the valuable input of some very close confidants. My friends Titus, Curt and my Dad read the original story in 2002 and encouraged me throughout the years to pick it back up and polish it off. When I completed the second draft, again they provided great input. Fellow author Ryan King guided me though the process of publishing, edited the final version and encouraged me to humble myself and put my writing out there. I am forever grateful these men helped and continue to help me realize this dream.

2320 HOURS, 22 OCTOBER 1998 – VIDNOYE, MOSKOVSKAYA OBLAST, RUSSIA

Oleg Komanitov Sergeiovich had never been called to work this late in the evening. Something had to be wrong, but the half liter of Vodka warming his gut was taking the immediacy out of the situation. The office was really a large shipping warehouse only a few blocks from the bar where they had been drinking in celebration of a recent job well done. Despite the wet cold, Oleg convinced Kolya to walk with him. After dealing with whatever was wrong at the office, maybe they could find some trouble. Kolya was always good for finding trouble. Good old Kolya.

"It's never this cold this time of year, Kolya. Damn this cold!"

"Da."

Although good for trouble, Kolya never said much.

"It was cold like this in the Korengal."

"Da."

"We were drunk most of the time back then, too."

"Da."

"Ah, Kolya! Good old days! Remember when we went into that village outside Asadabad to find those dirty Mujahedin who got Viktor?"

"Da. Koneshna."

"Kolya, try the English. The American will probably be at the office again. These days it is like he runs the crew. He pays good, that guy, but his neckties! My God, Kolya! All Americans have style like this now? Not like the old days."

"Da. Koneshna.....Yes, of course."

"Yes, the old days. That was a good time. We sent the goat fuckers to their god. Allahu Akhbar, goat fuckers! Their mothers, sons, daughters, and wives as well. But not before we had our way with them. And you poisoned

1

the well on the way out! Brilliant!"

"Da..yes. Ochen horosho...Very good. The old days. Spetsnaz. Special Forces."

As they rounded the corner and the warehouse came into sight, Oleg slipped on a patch of ice.

"It's never this cold this time of year, Kolya. Damn this cold! We move somewhere warm after a few more jobs, yes?"

"Da."

When they arrived at the main dock of the warehouse they had always simply called 'The Office', Oleg banged the cold corrugated door four times followed by two swift kicks.

"It's Oleg and Kolya," he yelled, "Let us in out of this damn cold!"

The door opened from the bottom and a rush of warm air hit their feet. It opened waist high and the two men bent over and entered. When Oleg stood up, he addressed the room in Russian; "What's so important that you drag me and Kolya out of our bar?"

Dmitriy, as usual, was sitting as the rest stood. "Speak English tonight, Oleg. We have company," the fat underboss said as he motioned toward the American. Despite the cold, Dmitriy was soaked with flop sweat. Oleg knew this wasn't because Dmitriy was nervous; he was just a fat bag of shit.

Oleg glared at Dmitriy and switched to English, "What is so important that you drag me and Kolya out of our bar?"

"We have a job for you," answered Dmitriy, "and you leave in the morning."

Oleg shook his head. "I just got back from a job, and if you remember, it wasn't easy and I haven't been paid yet."

Dmitriy tsk'ed and waved his hand in dismissal. "This one pays more, and we've always paid you, Oleg. Stop whining. We need you because this is important." Dmitriy pointed at the American. Oleg noted the garish tie around the American's neck and wrinkled his nose.

Oleg knew the American always paid well, but this particular situation was irregular and Oleg didn't like it. He had just returned from a job in the Caucasus securing a drug smuggling route from Afghanistan straight into a port in Azerbaijan. He was due payment, and he'd planned on retiring after receiving a couple more payments like these.

"How much?" Oleg snorted.

"You want to know what the job is?" asked Dmitriy.

Oleg shrugged and asked, "Does it matter?"

"No." Everyone turned their attention to the American who had replied in place of Dmitriy. "The payment is substantial. Coupled with your payment for establishing the smuggling route to Azerbaijan, your payday will be enough for retirement," the American motioned to Kolya, "for you both."

Kolya spoke up, "What is job?"

The American strolled to the table and placed his hands on an oversize Halliburton aluminum case. "You take this case to Belgium. Then drive a proscribed route and drop it off with my man in Luxembourg. Use the usual protocol."

"What is in case?" Kolya had become more talkative than usual.

Oleg noticed Yuri and Vyacheslav inch around behind he and Kolya. Something was odd here, thought Oleg. He took a few small steps toward the table where the American stood over the case.

The American lifted the lid. Oleg's eyes widened and his jaw dropped. In the middle of black foam casing sat a small ring of metal. It was rough and unpolished. It was dull gray with slight bronze streaks, and about the size of a large bracelet an ancient Egyptian queen might have worn.

"Nyet!" Oleg's panic caused a lapse back into Russian. He directed his immediate hysteria to Dmitriy, "Nyet, Dmitriy, nyet! I know what this is! Have you lost your mind? This is not normal! This is dangerous and foolish!"

Dmitriy folded his hands and turned to the American.

"So you won't take this job?" asked the American.

"Nyet!" Oleg shouted.

The American repeated the question in Russian, "So you won't take this job?"

"Nyet!"

"Suit yourself," the American smiled and closed the case. He took a few steps toward Dmitriy, who hadn't taken his eyes off the American. Oleg's eyes followed the American as he settled behind the underboss and placed his hands on Dmitriy's shoulders. Dmitriy looked up at Oleg, shook his head and said, "Goodbye, Tovarisch."

The American nodded his head once. Oleg took one step toward the American and began yelling, "Fuck your moth...."

In one sharp crack, Oleg's brain matter, skull fragments and blood sprayed across the table and onto the wall behind. Vyacheslav lowered his pistol and turned to Kolya.

Brushing bits of bone off his jacket and tie, the American yelled, "How about you? You interested?"

Kolya turned from Vyacheslav and looked at the American.

"Da. Pochyemu nyet? Sure. Why not?"

"Good. Come here. Take off your coat and roll up your right sleeve."

Kolya looked down at what remained of Oleg's face and regarded it for a moment. He shrugged and reached down to roll up his right coat sleeve as he walked toward the American.

MOGADISHU, SOMALIA

"Take point on this one, Quinn," the operator whispered.

Four dark shapes stacked behind him, each with rifle in one hand and each with their free hand on the shoulder of the man in front. He took three deep breaths, and nodded his head. Another dark shape stepped directly in front of the tin door, kicked and backed away. The flimsy tin flew off the hinges and landed in the center of the room. Quinn charged in and swept right, the next man swept left, the next forward. Quinn spotted three mats on the floor with three bodies stirring from the sudden commotion. Instead of shooting, he flopped on the closest body and put a knee in the chest of a malnourished black man. Seeing his lead, an operator and a Ranger subdued the other two persons in similar fashion. When the man he seized began to yell, Quinn put a gloved hand over the man's mouth and surveyed the rest of the room.

He heard someone say 'clear!' in a loud whisper.

Another loud whisper came from the far side of the single room tin shack, "Good call, Quinn. Shots would've brought the Sammies right down on us. Tie these fuckers up and gag them. Set up a perimeter and cover all sides. Price and I will get on the roof of this shack, lay out IR strobes and try to reestablish comms."

The two operators exited the shack, taking the tin door with them. They propped the broken door at the entrance and stacked some rubbish in front of it to keep the flimsy and rusty metal in place.

They tied the two men and the woman with their remaining zip ties, and cut strips off their dirty brown undershirts to use as gags. Once the three were tied, they piled them in a corner facing inward. The three Rangers then set up the best perimeter they could manage, covering four cardinal directions with three sets of eyes.

Sunrise was coming. Although it was October, at this latitude the sun came up at 0545. All had been quiet for hours with the exception of the sporadic fighting happening about a kilometer away where the 10th Mountain Division was still trying to exfil wounded and dead.

It was dead dark inside the room. The moon was lighting the street, but there wasn't anything stirring this early. Occasionally, moans or frustrated grunts would come from the three Sammies tied up in the corner. All he could think about was the coming sunlight and the inevitable fighting. This was over for most of his buddies, but not for the men in and on top of this shack.

Eventually, sunlight started to creep into the streets and into the holes serving as windows for the shack. Quinn was in a daze of exhaustion when one of their captives began to struggle against the zip ties, wailing as best she could against the gag.

Quinn left his position covering West and South to put an end to the racket. He brought his booted foot into the woman's chest and put the muzzle of his M4 in her face. She stopped the muffled wail and dipped her head.

Wait a second, Quinn thought.

He put the flash suppressor under her chin and brought her head up. With the sunlight creeping in the windows, he took a close look at her face. He studied the infuriated eyes for a moment, then studied the head scarf that had been pushed down around her neck. Rust orange with green streaks.

He whipped out his TL-122B angled flashlight and moved to the next captive. Quinn grabbed the man's gaunt face with one hand and shined the light in his face. He studied it for a moment and moved to the next man to do the same. He backed away slowly, staring at all three in disgust.

"Newton," he whispered.

"Yes, sergeant?

"Check this out."

He shined the flashlight on the three.

"Looks like three strung out Sammies to me, Sergeant," Newton whispered.

It's not an easy choice. Kill them, young man. You have to do it on your own.

Time stood still for a brief moment as that queer familiar voice, almost a whisper, pierced the moment. This wasn't the first time Quinn heard the voice.

Quinn shook his head against the voice and whispered, "Man, don't you remember yesterday when that mob passed us while we were watching the D-boys' backs? These three were there! This one here," Quinn pointed at one of the men, "was dragging that guy by his heel, and this one here," he pointed his rifle at the other man, "was stomping on the guy's dead body. And this one," Quinn took two steps and took a knee, bringing his face an inch from the woman's, "cut the guy's pants off then sliced his dick and balls off."

Newton was silent for a moment then whispered, "Dude, they all look the same to me. I was pissing myself when they passed us, anyway."

It's them, son. No mistake. They don't live another day. They'd do the same to you or your sister and you know it. You know it's right. Stop thinking and do it.

No, no. He knew no one in that shack said those words. That wasn't how it happened.

"It's them," Quinn said.

If you don't want to bring the bad guys down on you, you can always just cut their throats. Field expedient justice. You can do this, Joshua.

"So what should we do, sergeant?" Newton asked.

Three light taps on the tin roof signaled the Rangers to hold it down.

Quinn thought for a moment, then whispered back, "Well we can't just let them go. I saw what they did. They dragged those guys through the streets and..."

"There were more of them than just three," Newton whispered.

"I know that, but," he stopped speaking when he heard what sounded like a technical driving by outside.

The next time there's a loud noise outside, do what you have to do.

The fighting would begin again soon, so there's always that opportunity. Wait. I thought that, but no one said it....

"Newton," he whispered, "what should we do about these..."

Then a low whine pierced the air, followed by the low pitched buzz of a 7.62 mini-gun. The sound of RPG tubes firing answered the buzz, then repeating small arms fire. It had begun again.

"Ah shit," Newton said aloud, "Here we go again. Sergeant, I don't know if that's them or not, but do what you gotta do and get back to your corners."

Throughout the entire hushed conversation, he hadn't taken his eyes off the three captives. There was more gunfire outside. The technical had found its way back to the shack, and Newton was holding them off the best he could as the operators on the roof called in air support. He took two steps closer to the captives.

Do it. It's right. It's justice. Do it, son.

He brought the muzzle of his M4 to the temple of the first man and pulled the trigger. He moved to the second man's face and pulled the trigger. The woman, horrified and struggling against her restraints, was writhing in the blood of the two men. He moved the muzzle from her head to her gut and pulled the trigger four times. As she screamed against the gag in the fetal position, he returned to his corners, firing at the enemy approaching from the west and the south.

Well done, young man.

No one said that. It was too loud to hear anything.

Suddenly, the roof opened and he was floating up. He landed in a room with two men in suits. He was sitting in a chair, his hands cuffed behind him. This wasn't how it happened! The fighting went on for another day!

"You're in big trouble, son," one of the men said. "We're investigating you for crimes against humanity. You've violated the Geneva Convention, and you can plan on a very lengthy jail sentence."

He struggled against his handcuffs until his wrists bled. He didn't remember any of this. When did this happen?

Three deep buzzes shook the room. The criminal investigators didn't seem to notice.

"Son, you shot three unarmed civilians," one the men said.

Civilians? You see this horse malarkey, Joshua?

No. They weren't civilians.

Buzzes shook the room again, and a ceiling tile fell on the table in front of him.

The other investigator leaned over the table, took Josh by his dusty body armor and screamed, "You're going to Leavenworth when everyone finds out about this. Newton will talk."

I did the right thing. Justice was served.

Justice was served. They started this war. You ended it.

Another three buzzes. This time they knocked him to the floor, chair and all.

None of this happened!

0400 HOURS, 24 OCTOBER 1998 – BIAMONT, SOIGNIES, BELGIUM

Bzzzz! Bzzzz! Bzzzz!

Joshua Quinn awoke on the cold wood floor in a fit of thrashing. He jerked his head up and looked at the bed out of which he'd just fallen and let out a sound that was not quite a scream and not quite a moan. He was covered in sweat and panting. For the fifth time in two months, the pager was buzzing at 0400 on the dot. He threw off the sticky sheets and blanket and reached up to his bed stand to retrieve the pager. The code read '7777', which meant, 'Get to headquarters immediately'. He put his legs under himself and lumbered off the floor.

Muttering in the darkness, Josh shuffled to the shower. He turned on the water and waited for it to warm a bit. "What is it this time?" He asked aloud, "Piss test? Early accountability formation? Weapons cleaning? Surprise responsiveness drill? What?" He whipped a towel off the rack and struck his funny bone on the sink. Perfect start, he thought as he rubbed his elbow and stepped in the shower.

As he shaved, Josh realized he had managed only three hours of sleep. He had been up late finishing the evaluation reports of the last surveillance exercise his unit conducted. The night before, he had been up until 0200 finishing his own Non-Commissioned Officer Evaluation Report. That was due today, as well. The night before that, he was tasked to run a night fire weapons range and didn't get home until 0130. Was it Friday already? It didn't matter. Whatever this nonsense with the page was about, he'd be filling out paperwork all weekend. At least in 75th Ranger Regiment, there wasn't as much paperwork. Military intelligence seemed to be more about paperwork and procedure than actually collecting information, or in Josh's case; countering the enemy collecting information.

Josh tore out of his parking space at 0435. If he wasn't at work by 0500, he was bound to get an ass chewing. He had to take the corners a little slower than usual due to the icy spots, but on the straights he floored it. He saw the flash of the speed camera as he did every fourth or fifth trip to the office. There's another one, thought Josh. Paying traffic fines was taking a big chunk of his meager E-6 income here in Belgium.

At 0458, according to the dashboard second hand clock on the dashboard of his '88 Opal, Josh pulled into the office parking lot. He shielded his face from the sleet and ran toward the building. He swiped his badge and entered the key code. Didn't work. He swiped and entered the code again. Didn't work. He banged on the door a few times and waited. No one. He banged and waited. No one. He repeated the process a number of times for the next 15 minutes until Captain Beebe opened the door.

"Morning, sir," said Josh as he brushed passed the company commander.

"About damn time, staff sergeant," the captain shot back.

"Yes, sir. I'm here. What's up, sir?"

"Mission brief in the conference room, but I'd like to speak to you in my office before you go in."

"Yes, sir," said Josh.

Captain Clovis Xavier Beebe IV turned on his heel and marched to his office with Josh in tow. Now what? He's going to bitch me out about something. No day was complete without a Beebe ass chewing. It was tough getting a daily ass chewing by a guy only a year older than you, thought Josh.

Captain Beebe opened his office door and allowed Josh to enter before him. He closed the door behind him. It's going to be one of *those*, Josh thought.

"Have a seat, Staff Sergeant," said Beebe as he made his way around his massive oak desk.

Josh settled in the seat to the right of the desk. At least from this angle, he didn't have to look at the Beebe's West Point diploma and class picture. No matter what the angle, the glint off his massive class ring couldn't be missed. He always tapped it against the desk as he spoke.

"Staff Sergeant, you're my acting First Sergeant. Are you not?"

"I am, sir."

Beebe rustled some papers, looked at them, then tossed them aside. The ass chewing thus began; "You certainly aren't acting the part. I've identified at least four deficiencies in your duties, the most egregious being your inaccurate quarterly inventory." Tap, tap, tap.

"'Egregious', sir?" Josh knew what the word meant; he just wanted to let Beebe know he didn't need to use big words.

"Bad. Particularly bad. The worst." Tap, tap, tap, tap.

"How so, sir? The quarterly inventory was executed in the same manner as the last four inventories." Josh was genuinely puzzled.

"Exactly!" shouted Beebe, "That equipment; the radios and the handsets are still missing!"

"Yes, sir. That equipment was missing when you took command last year. We've written it up as a loss."

"I signed that hand receipt without knowing the equipment was missing, and now battalion is looking for the equipment," said Beebe.

"Sir, I told you--"

Beebe waved his finger at Josh, "No you didn't! No you didn't. You were signed for that equipment before I signed for it. I am calling for a Financial Liability Investigation of Property Loss and a subsequent statement of charges. You are now financially liable for that equipment. Unless it is found before the next quarterly inventory, you will pay for it."

Josh was stunned. He had told Beebe about the missing equipment and had warned him not to sign the hand receipt over until it was found or tracked. At the time, Beebe was so excited to have his first command that he disregarded everything Josh had told him about company operations and equipment. Josh had been around officers like this for about six years now. There was no winning this one and he'd have to pay. His hands started to tremble a bit, but he answered levelly. "Yes, sir."

"So you accept liability, Sergeant?" asked Beebe.

"Sure, sir. Why not?"

"Let's watch that military bearing, Sergeant."

So it was Sergeant now. By the end of this conversation, Josh would be a private again.

"Now on to the other infractions."

"Sir, isn't there a mission brief in the conference room?"

"That can wait, Sergeant," said Beebe, "there may be an operation, but this is still my surveillance company and they can wait for me."

"Yes, sir."

"As I was saying, " tap, tap, tap, "your infractions and shortcomings."

Josh joined his trembling hands in his lap and bit the side of his tongue.

Tap, tap, tap, tap, tap, "Did you know Specialists Nieman and Pohl recently tested positive for THC on their last urinalysis?"

"No, sir. When was the urinalysis? I wasn't aware they were tested."

"It was a week ago. You see, Sergeant? That's my point Specialists Nieman and Pohl are *your* soldiers. You had no idea they were tested, and you had no idea they tested positive."

Josh looked down at his hands and shook his head.

"Sergeant?" Tap, tap, tap, "Do you have something to say? Your commanding officer is addressing you."

Josh curled his toes and flexed his calves until they cramped. Only then could he speak in a level tone, "Sir, Specialists Nieman and Pohl are both in the detachment office in Bamberg. That's a day's drive from here, and I've been on mission for the last month. When I call to speak to Specialists Nieman and Pohl, the detachment commander won't allow them to speak to me. 'It's undermining his authority,' he says. Sir, I can't manage soldiers' lives from here."

"Those sound like complaints and excuses to me, Sergeant," said Beebe through constant taps. "You should have found time to counsel those soldiers on drug use."

"And that would have stopped them smoking pot?" asked Josh.

"It would have covered you. Now I will formally give you a written counseling on not properly counseling your soldiers. This will be your third such counseling, and I will be forced to execute non-judicial punishment on you. Article 15." Tap, tap, tap.

Captain Beebe proceeded to outline Josh's deficiencies. The style of his surveillance reports was unacceptable. The format of his evaluation report was unacceptable. Being 15 minutes late for work this morning was unacceptable. Excessive traffic fines are unacceptable. The list went on and so did the promises for further non-judicial punishment unless Josh cleaned up his act. Only when the surveillance team's senior chief warrant officer interrupted the meeting thirty minutes later to tell Beebe they needed to begin the briefing did the ass chewing session end.

Josh left the office behind Beebe and Chief Smith thinking this one meeting had lightened his wallet a good six grand. His calf ached from the flexing, and he had drawn blood from his tongue. His shirt was stuck to his body under his sport coat. None of this was from fear or humiliation or shame. It wasn't right. None of this was right.

They walked down the hall and made a right into the conference room. Inside there were more people than Josh expected. Usually, only a handful of agents were present for the surveillance mission briefs. This time, there were at least twelve. Josh recognized a few of them; agents from the neighboring field offices in The Netherlands and Germany. Everyone was exchanging greetings and comparing recent war stories from the field. These were mostly warrant officers--they had ignored Captain Beebe's entrance, much to the obvious distaste of the Company Commander. Beebe seated himself at the head of the conference table with a sullen look on his face. He glared at a few of the warrants engaged in their own conversations with other warrants. They were obviously waiting for someone.

Josh spoke only to Staff Sergeant Tyler from the field office in The Hague. He had received his page at 0100 and some of the guys from the German field offices had received pages even earlier. He pressed Tyler for information about the situation and the brief, but he knew even less than Josh.

At 0630, Chief Smith quieted the room and gave the initial brief. At 1100, the team would be conducting a surveillance, target unknown. Chief Smith said the Surveillance Controller, or Sierra Charlie, would arrive in a few minutes to give more details. Chief Smith excused himself and left the room. The room again became a din of speculation and indignant questions.

"Three and a half hours to prepare for a surveillance mission?"

"What kind of surveillance will this be?"

"Who is the Sierra Charlie?"

"Did you know anything about this?"

"Who is the target? Russians? Iranians? Hezbollah?"

"Six teams of two?"

"Where is the equipment?"

"What vehicles are we using?"

Being one of the youngest and least experienced agents in the room, Josh sat back and listened. He didn't care about the questions and speculation. So far, this was one of the coolest things that had happened in his career in military intelligence--little notice, little information, little time to plan, and very mysterious. This could actually be *real*. Plus there was the added bonus of being back on mission and away from the extraneous administrative bullshit. Perhaps he'd forget about the promised non-judicial punishment courtesy of Beebe.

The sidebar conversations and theories continued for several minutes, some becoming heated. Josh was the only one who noticed the man ease in through the back door of the conference room. The man surveyed the room, listened to the conversations, calculating every individual. Although he had obviously paid two grand more for his suit than anyone in this room, there was something else subtly different about him.

He was about 6 feet tall, 190 to 200 pounds, early 40s, dark hair with gray streaks, blue eyes, five o'clock shadow, fifty dollar haircut, and a measuring demeanor. But what was it that was different? Josh couldn't put his finger on it. In the 75th Ranger Regiment, he had worked with guys that carried themselves in this fashion. This guy was obviously the surveillance controller, or Sierra Charlie, and Josh could tell he had been there and done that. His eyes shifted from person to person. When his eyes finally met Josh's, the man winked at Josh and cleared his throat.

"Excuse me, gentlemen," he began, "Thank you for responding to the call so quickly. If you'll give me a few moments to explain the mission today, I'd appreciate it. Please be seated and save your questions."

His voice had an air of unquestioning authority and expertise. Everyone quickly and quietly found a chair around the table and sat, attention focused on the man in the thousand dollar suit. He continued to survey the room, eyes still moving from person to person. His eyes settled on Captain Beebe, who remained seated at the head of the table. Josh noticed Beebe's sullen look had taken on a judgmental quality as he stared back at the Sierra Charlie. They glared at each other for an uncomfortable moment.

The man spoke first; "Sir? Will you excuse us?"

"Excuse you?" Beebe asked incredulously.

"Yes. Excuse us," the man answered back immediately, "unless you're cleared for Indigo Branch. I believe everyone in here but you is cleared for this special access program."

"Uh," Beebe was obviously confused. "Uh, I'm not familiar with that program."

The man walked to the door and opened it. "Then you'll excuse us?"

Beebe had gone from sullen to judging to confused to humiliated in a matter of moments. He collected his papers and shuffled to the door. As Beebe eased around the man and out the door with his head down, the man thanked him and promptly shut the door. When the man turned back into the room, Josh could see him smirking

Seeing Beebe humiliated was heaven for Josh, but when he realized he'd never heard of Indigo Branch himself, he realized he'd have to excuse himself as well. Just as Josh was about to stand and make his way out, the man spoke up again.

"Now that he's out of the way, we can get down to business."

The room erupted in laughs. The man let the group laugh and nudge one another for a few moments, then he began, "My name is Bradley Dorne, and I'll be the Sierra Charlie for the surveillance mission later this morning. The target, Zulu 1, is Kolya Aliyev, Russian Organized Crime. Up front, I suspect him of trafficking advanced weapon components in order to sell them on the black market somewhere in Western Europe. He landed in Brussels under an assumed name yesterday afternoon. I've been tracking this guy for the better part of a year, and he's never been this far west. I have no idea why he's here in Belgium. It doesn't fit his group's pattern and that's why we're going to follow him today. This will be a preventative surveillance. I want him to know we're watching him."

A few of the older agents around the table muttered to themselves. A preventative surveillance was never much fun, and was oftentimes very boring. The dissatisfaction wasn't lost on Dorne.

"I know, gentlemen. I know. Maybe we'll get lucky and he'll screw up. I have the authority to make an arrest, but hopefully it won't come to that. I'm hoping he'll pick us up early and go right back to the airport and fly back to Moscow. "

Chief Frederickson, one of the older agents, spoke up; "Will we be armed, Mr. Dorne?"

"Certainly," said Dorne. "Aliyev will be traveling with three armed thugs: Zulus 2, 3, and 4. They call themselves his protective detail, but they're nothing more than gorillas. We'll be armed because it will be better to have them and not need them than to need them and not have them against these thugs. Question answered?"

Everyone nodded in agreement.

"Great," he continued, "Target vehicle, X-Ray 1, is a 1997 black Mercedes S class. At around 1100, we'll be picking up X-ray 1 at the La Roseraie Hotel just outside Brussels. Again, I have no idea where he's going, but I do know he'll be leaving at 1100. I have secured clearance for you gentlemen to travel cross border as long as he stays in Belgium, France, The Netherlands, and Germany. We'll follow him as long as it takes to determine his intent."

Frederickson spoke up again; "And what if he does go into a country you didn't mention?"

"I'll worry about that when the time comes," Dorne said. "Just take all your commands from the tower. I am the tower. Understood?"

Frederickson nodded.

Dorne continued, "I have secured seven vehicles and comms packages for each. Body comms are in the trunk. Wire them up, as well. You decide amongst yourselves who will be drivers and who will be navigators based on your skill levels. I will be riding alone in the black van, which will be the Sierra Charlie vehicle."

More muttering from the older agents. It was very unusual for a surveillant to be one-up; alone in other words. It was even more unusual, irresponsible even, for a Sierra Charlie to be one-up. Dorne ignored the muttering.

"Right. So if there aren't any questions, I will pass around information packets which include maps and photographs of X-ray 1 and Zulus 1, 2, 3, and 4. Draw your weapons from the arms room, but do it quickly. Comms are already hooked up in the vehicles. Vehicles are outside the office around the corner. Comms check in 15 minutes. Hook up your body comms on the way. Rendezvous at La Roseraie Hotel at 1000 hours. I'll set the box once we establish comms at the rendezvous point."

Dorne strode out of the room through the back door before anyone had a chance to ask a question.

Almost everyone in the room looked at their watches simultaneously. 0658. After the comms check, they'd have just under three hours to get to Brussels. Not much time at all, thought Josh. He gathered his notes and made his way out the door where he was confronted by a very flustered Captain Beebe.

Josh had seen this version of Beebe many times. Young Captains screw up a lot, and their superiors often chastise them daily. Beebe's go-to after being chastised in any way was to take it out on the lowest ranking soldier he happened to come across. In almost every case, this soldier was Staff

Sergeant Joshua D. Quinn. Chief Smith seemed to see what was coming, and he came to Josh's side.

Beebe was fingering his class ring. Not a good sign. "Sergeant, I don't think it's a good idea for you to be armed."

"Sir--" Chief Smith began. Beebe cut him off with a wave of his hand.

"I won't hear it, Mr. Smith. That is my arms room. Sergeant Quinn has amply demonstrated he is not fit to be armed. I will not risk an international incident by having this...soldier armed for this mission."

Josh bit his lip so hard he drew blood.

"Furthermore," Beebe continued, "I'm not sure he's fit for this surveillance mission..."

Beebe's words started to fade as the ringing in Josh's ears grew louder and louder. The metallic taste in his mouth only amplified the ringing. He lowered his head and swallowed, trying to focus on the patterns in the linoleum floor. The vision in his left eye began to blur. He shook his head to bring his vision back, but a dull pain began to manifest behind that left eye. Josh couldn't hear the yelling match between Chief Smith and Beebe over the intense ringing. He barely noticed Chief Smith take him by the arm to walk him down the hall and out the back of the office into the wet Belgian morning.

Chief Smith led Josh around the corner toward the vehicles. The ringing had begun to fade, but the vision in his left eye was still blurry. Smith released his arm and said, "Go wire up your body comms, Quinn. You're in the blue Citroen. And don't let the CO get to you. Focus on the mission today."

Josh's barely heard a word Smith said. His jaw ached and the pain behind his eyes was intensifying. He spit blood on the wet pavement and started toward the blue Citroen. Tyler was there wiring himself up with the body comms.

"Goddam, Quinn," Tyler said as Josh approached the Citroen, "what did you do to piss off Beebe? Goddam!"

The vision in Josh's left eye suddenly went completely black. He saw only blood red out of his right eye. The ringing was now so loud he couldn't think. He clenched his jaw so tight it felt as if his teeth might shatter. Without warning Josh reared his head back, yelled and kicked the passenger side door. The window shattered and the plastic paneling caved in. His vision immediately cleared and the ringing was gone. The pain behind his eyes was gone. All Josh could sense was the light rain falling on his head, and the metallic taste of blood. He looked around and saw the team members' shocked stares. He glanced from person to person; Chief Smith, Chief Frederickson, Tyler, Perry, and the rest.

A piercing whistle broke the silence. Josh spun around and saw Dorne standing next to a black passenger van.

"Change of plans," he yelled. "You're riding with me, Quinn."

0730 hours, 24 October 1998 – La Roseraie Hotel, Brussels, Belgium

More than once Kolya Aliyev had awakened to the sight of a dead prostitute, but never two dead prostitutes.

"Shit," he muttered. The last thing he remembered from the previous evening was snorting a line of cocaine just as the hookers arrived. It had been quite a task to acquire cocaine just after landing in Brussels, but he had always been resourceful when it came to narcotics. Now he needed to be resourceful in getting rid of these bodies. He leaned down to examine the peroxide blonde. Just like before--heavy bruising around the throat. He then staggered to the brunette. "Hmm," he murmured as he rolled her over. The whites of her lifeless eyes were black. Heavy hemorrhaging. He had obviously beaten her to death. He titled his head as he looked at the dead, black eyes. "Shit," he muttered again. This might complicate things.

Kolya shook his head against the pounding hangover headache. He grabbed a bottle of something and took a swig as he made his way to the bathroom. He splashed some water on his face and looked in the mirror. His right cheek was caked with dried blood. He'd need a shower. He turned on the water and took another swig.

When he stepped out of the shower, he heard his Iridium satellite phone ringing. He dried himself off and went to answer it.

"Da."

"English, please." It was the American.

"Yes."

"I'm calling to make sure you're sober enough to do this today."

"I am sober," Kolya replied.

"Good. I want you go alone today. Don't take Vyacheslav and Yuri. They attract too much attention."

"Why is this? Is not normal," Kolya said as he again grabbed a handful of the brunette's hair and again examined the dead eyes.

"Kolya, just do as you're told. You don't need them today. Send them back to Moscow."

"Yes. I understand." Kolya shook his head, and released the handful of hair. The woman's head hit the floor with a thud.

"Good. You understand the rest of the plan?"

"Yes."

"Stick to it. Proceed with the rest as planned." The phone went dead.

"Yeb t'voy maht!" Kolya yelled into the Iridium. He tossed it on the bed and picked up the hotel phone. He called Vyacheslav and then Yuri. He told them to catch a taxi back to the airport, and fly back to Moscow tonight. When he hung up with Yuri, he glanced at the alarm clock on the night stand. 0815. Just under three hours to get rid of these bodies. He glanced at the Halliburton case and saw it was spattered with dried blood. He'd have to clean off that case, too. Kolya sighed as he took the blonde by the ankles and dragged her off the bed. The woman's armed flopped on the case as her body hit the floor. Kolya dropped her legs and stared at the case for a moment. What was ten percent of $36 million? That's it: by the day's end, he'd be $3.6 million richer.

0800 HOURS, 24 OCTOBER 1998 – E19 EXPRESSWAY, BELGIUM

"Just merge onto the 19," Dorne said from the back of the van.

Josh gently guided the van toward the E19 on-ramp. Traffic was going to be a pain. The 60 kilometer trip might take two hours or more.

Neither Josh nor Dorne had addressed the outburst just before they left the motor pool. Dorne had simply tossed Josh the keys and told him to drive. He hadn't had time to review the packet, the maps, the photographs, or wire up his body comms. He'd been sheepishly asking for directions as Dorne busied himself in the back of the van. There was a thin curtain between the cab and the back of the van, so Josh couldn't see exactly what Dorne was doing back there. According to the clicks, hums, and the twitches of the voltmeter on the dashboard, he was furiously activating multiple electronic systems. Then, a familiar yet menacing sound--Dorne charged a round into the breach of a handgun. He whipped back the curtain, swung around and settled in the passenger seat.

"Ahhh!" he sighed as he pulled the seatbelt over his shoulder, "not as young as springtime anymore. Whew!" He turned his head to Josh and offered him a pistol, butt first. "It's charged," Dorne said.

Josh looked at the pistol for a moment, and then accepted it. He checked the safety and slid it under his right thigh. "Thanks," he said. "This thing isn't military issue, is it?"

"You're military and I issued it to you. So it's military issue," returned Dorne.

Josh smiled at the comment. "Yes, sir."

Dorne crinkled his nose as if he had whiffed a stiff fart. "Listen kid, call me 'Brad' or 'Dorne'. No 'sirs'."

"Alright. Dorne, then." Josh kept his smile. He liked this guy.

"Tell me something, Joshua," Dorne said. Josh could feel it coming. He'd have to explain his behavior back at the motor pool. "You're a Ranger, aren't you?"

Josh just nodded his head yes. The question had caught him a bit off guard. He tried to keep that to himself in the MI community. Once MI guys knew they had a Ranger in their midst, they always needed to somehow prove that they were either as high speed as the Ranger, or more often; smarter than the Ranger. Josh suspected his being a former infantryman was one of the reasons Beebe had it out for him. MI officers were always intimidated by infantrymen.

"That's what I thought," Dorne said. "I could tell by the way you tucked the pistol under your thigh, butt out, and at the ready. Not a lot of non-Rangers would do that. They'd think they'd shoot their balls off." Dorne chuckled to himself, "Damn Joshua, how do you work with these guys?"

Again, Josh was a bit confused. Dorne was one of 'these guys', wasn't he? Since he'd been in Europe, Josh had worked with a few shadowy CIA and FBI types. They never revealed exactly for whom they worked, but if they were working with Josh's surveillance team, they had something to do with the intelligence community. Josh hadn't had time to think about who Dorne was or for whom he worked. He talked the talk, so he must be legit. Probably CIA, but no CIA agent carried himself the way Dorne did. It was protocol in the intelligence community not to pry when one worked with these shadowy guys, but Josh pressed his luck: "Were you at Regiment, Dorne?"

"Nope, but I've worked with them," replied Dorne, "but it seems like a long time ago, now." Dorne turned around and brushed the curtain aside. He pulled out what looked like a miniature laptop computer. He turned back in his seat and opened the computer. The screen immediately came up. Josh had a hard time keeping his eyes on the road. He'd never seen a laptop that small, let alone with a high resolution color screen. A map on the screen was scrolling in real time, and images looked like satellite photography. Dorne zoomed in on a blue blip on the map, and back out to five other blue blips in a line moving southeast to northwest. Josh realized the line was the E19, and the blue blips were the surveillance team's vehicles. Dorne swept his finger across the screen, then up at a 90 degree angle. The map panned out and a bright stationary yellow blip appeared northwest of the line of blue blips. Dorne didn't look up as he calmly said, "Eyes on the road, Joshua."

Josh looked up just in time to lightly tap the brakes and avoid rear-ending a semi-trailer. "Sorry," Josh said.

"No problem," said Dorne, still looking at the screen, "you've probably never seen technology like this, have you?"

"I haven't," answered Josh, "I've only heard of stuff like that."

Dorne snapped the computer closed. "Then you're in for some treats today, buddy. But we have some time to chat now before we get to the La Roseraie. I have a few questions for you, Joshua."

"Alright."

"First tell me this," Dorne said, "how long have you been dealing with your problem?"

"Which problem is that?" asked Josh, perfectly aware of the problem Dorne addressed was the outburst at the motor pool.

"Let's not do that, Joshua," replied Dorne. "Just tell me how long you've been dealing with your violent outbursts."

Josh looked down for a moment. How long had he been dealing with the flare-ups? No one had ever bothered to ask him the simple question Dorne had just asked. Josh explained he'd always had a temper, but he could usually take it out on the football field or the wrestling mat in junior high and high school. Every time he lost his temper and had an outburst, he had the same symptoms: headaches, the loss of vision, and the ringing in his ears. He nearly lost his football scholarship at Southwest Texas State due to a bar fight, and that was the first real manifestation of negative consequences due to his rage.

"What was the fight about?" Dorne asked.

Josh told him an abbreviated version of the story: Some drunken frat boy had shoved a woman to the floor. Josh demanded the guy apologize, and the fight ensued. The next incident was a bit more serious. "Tell me about it." Dorne said.

Josh was at a post-graduation party he and his friends had organized at a local haunt in San Marcos. He was also celebrating his acceptance into the Texas Tech School of Law. The party was winding down, and he and his friends were filtering out into the parking lot. Three Hispanic men were in the parking lot drinking near Josh's car. As Josh passed them, one of the men threw a bottle at Josh's feet and called him a name in Spanish. One of his buddies decided to give the men an earful. Josh turned around just in time to see one of the men break a bottle over his buddy's head. Josh didn't remember much about the fight, but when the police and paramedics showed up to tend to the men Josh had beaten bloody, the police informed him one of the 'men' wasn't a man at all. The kid was only 16. Josh was arrested and charged with assault. Even in Texas, and even in extenuating circumstances such as these, you still couldn't beat up a minor without being charged by the State. Josh had never been arrested and charged before, so the judge went easy on him. The judge gave him the old 'go into the military or spend time in jail' sentence. Josh opted for enlistment. Given the circumstances, the only career field open was 11B: Light Infantry.

"Mm-hm," Dorne muttered. "Any problems in the military?"

Josh related a few minor incidents with peers, but he'd never had any incidents with his superiors. Just before he'd been selected to attend Ranger School, when he'd be getting chewed out for something minor, Josh could feel some of the same symptoms that preceded an outburst. Once he made it through Ranger School and into Regiment, he was too engaged to feel the anger. But all that changed in October 1993.

"Mogadishu," Dorne said with a nod. Josh thought he picked up a tone of nostalgia in Dorne's voice.

"Were you there?" asked Josh.

"Yes," replied Dorne, "but we can talk about me later. Tell me what changed."

Josh turned to get another look at Dorne, thinking he might be able to recognize him from his time in Somalia. Nothing about him looked familiar. "Well," said Josh, "if you were there, you know how it was those three days."

Dorne nodded, "Not many people realize the battle went on that long."

Josh told Dorne he had been on the initial ground convoy to the Olympic Hotel. He'd made Sergeant at this point, so he was a vehicle commander. After the first Black Hawk crashed, his vehicle along with three others were ordered to take wounded back to the airfield. His convoy made it back to the airfield, unloaded the wounded, then made their way back out into the city to provide exfil for the stranded Rangers. His convoy ended up four blocks from the Olympic hotel. By this point, the second Black Hawk had crashed and all hell had broken loose. Josh's convoy was given five sets of conflicting orders: Go back to airfield immediately, and /or; make their way to the first crash site and provide exfil for the Rangers there, and / or; make their way to the second crash site and provide exfil for the Rangers there, and / or; exfil wounded Rangers at another site two blocks from the Olympic Hotel, and / or; provide over-watch for a stranded Ranger chalk serving as a makeshift casualty collection point, or CCP, six blocks from the second crash site.

While trying to decide which orders to follow, two vehicles in Josh's convoy were hit by RPG and small arms fire and disabled. Since they were only a couple hundred feet from the makeshift CCP, Josh decided to follow the last set of orders. He collected the radios and sensitive items from the three disabled vehicles, collected the ammunition, destroyed the disabled vehicles with a thermite grenade, and then led his men to the CCP. When his men and the last functioning vehicle made it to the casualty collection point, it became apparent the Task Force had lost all control of the operation.

All twelve Rangers in the CCP were wounded including the senior non-commissioned officers, and six of the twelve were obviously expectant. The medic, whose left hand was completely bandaged, was doing his best to keep the NCOs alive. The radio operator was trying in vain to make sense of more conflicting orders coming from three separate commands while he placed tourniquets on what remained of his legs. Since he was the only functional NCO, everyone looked at Josh for leadership.

Dorne interrupted, "Stay on the E19. We're running ahead of schedule, so we're going the long way."

Josh veered back onto E19 and continued his story.

Josh took charge immediately. First he set up a perimeter in the concrete shack the CCP was using as a shelter, then he organized communications. There were three higher unit commands giving orders: Ranger command, 10th Mountain command, and JSOC who controlled the Delta operators and the overall mission. Josh tuned three different radios to the three different frequencies and had the radio operator monitor all three for fifteen minutes before responding to any orders any one of the three commands gave. This would establish a level of situational awareness and it would also establish which command would be the most responsive. During those fifteen minutes, the CCP was assaulted four times. All four times, Josh's Rangers repelled the attacks. Upon completion of the radio monitoring, Josh determined the most responsive command was JSOC. Josh then made a command decision to simply switch off the other two radios and take his commands from JSOC alone.

For the next two hours, Josh arranged for all the wounded to be exfil'ed back to the airfield via three vehicle convoy with an air escort. After the wounded had been exfil'ed Josh had four Rangers. JSOC told Josh there would not be another convoy to exfil them, and they were to make their way to a grid coordinate that was three blocks south of their current location.

Their three block journey took two hours. Josh lost one of his Rangers along the way. PFC Traynor stepped in front of a Somali Technical with a mounted anti-aircraft gun. The gun tore Traynor to pieces. Josh and his team took care of the Technical with their M-60 and thermite grenades, then gathered Traynor's remains--a hand, an upper thigh, the back of his skull, and his dog tags. They stowed Traynor's remains in Josh's drop sack and pressed forward.

When they arrived at the grid coordinate, they found two Delta operators waiting for them in a makeshift CP. The two operators were, in effect, coordinating the entire battle in the city. They had all three commands on the net. They were coordinating close air support, or CAS, calling in strafing runs for stranded Rangers, and arranging for exfil of wounded Rangers and Delta operators throughout the city. They instructed Josh and his Rangers to provide over-watch. Watching them work in between Somali assaults was a thing of beauty. They broke all the conventional rules while adhering to the laws of violence. They coordinated the impossible because they worked around the system while remaining inside it.

The group manned the CP and coordinated the battle throughout the night. From where Josh sat, he would have sworn they were winning this battle. By morning, the Blackhawk crews, dead or alive, were exfil'ed, and the helicopters had been destroyed. The Ranger task force was back at the airfield, and a few of the men supporting the Delta operators were tidying up the battle space by way of coordinating exfil for remaining operators who had been holed up most of the night.

Josh paused for a moment, then cleared his throat and continued his story.

At that point, the mission became personnel recovery. A few Somalis had decided to take the remains of dead soldiers in hopes of ransoming them. The group's orders were to recover the remains by any means necessary. The group of five ended up recovering the remains of two operators, four operator support personnel, and three Rangers. In the process, the group killed at least forty Somalis in close quarters combat.

The process of finding the bodies, arranging for exfil, and moving to the next target went on for the next 18 hours. Instead of sleeping, the group assigned one person to rest while they waited for exfil on each target.

Finally the order for their own exfil arrived. At 0300 hours on 5 October, a Black Hawk helicopter landed on a dirt soccer field and exfil'ed Josh and his Rangers. The operators remained behind to do God knows what.

When Josh and his team arrived back at the airfield, they realized the US had actually lost the Battle of Mogadishu.

"None of what you described was in the news or the books, was it?" Dorne asked.

"Not at all. It's still the most amazing thing to me," Josh replied.

"Does it bother you?" Dorne asked.

"Does what bother me?" Josh returned.

"That beyond the public demanding we pull out of Somalia, no one seemed to care. Does that bother you?"

Josh thought for a moment, then answered, "Of course it bothers me a bit. I don't exactly know what I was expecting when we landed back in Georgia when it was all said and done, but I quickly learned I wasn't expecting absolutely nothing. In the back of my mind I might have been imagining some sort of flag-waving welcome home as we got off the plane, complete with photographers and wives and kids running across the tarmac to hug and kiss their husbands and fathers. There was nothing like what you see in the movies from the 1940s. Of course it wasn't like Vietnam, either. No one was spitting on us or anything. On the bus ride back to base from the airport, I was overwhelmed by my country's apathy to what had just happened to me and my brothers."

Dorne nodded and said, "Even in 1993, everyone was at the mall."

Josh nodded in agreement. "That's a good way to put it. No one noticed what had really happened. No one noticed history was probably made in Mogadishu."

"How so?" Dorne asked.

"I'm no history scholar," Josh said, " but I can't think of a single example from history wherein a bone-breaking tactical defeat resulted in such a grand strategic victory. We took losses, but we kicked that city's teeth in for two straight days. We captured or killed our targets that day. All things considered we performed well, but once the US and international media sank their teeth into dead, naked soldiers being dragged through the streets along with those 18 flag draped coffins, our mission in Somalia was over. We pulled back and then out, and the warlords and whichever bad guys were supporting them won the strategic fight. Our enemies around the world began to see us differently. To this day, nothing changed over there. Plus with our enemies emboldened, the US was essentially less safe than before we arrived. I haven't watched much news since. I stick with the newspaper to keep me current."

"Mm-hm. Good observations," said Dorne, "but the media can be your friend as well as your enemy. Stay current, Joshua. That same media could be turned on its ear and work for you the same way it worked against us in the aftermath of that battle."

Josh cocked his head and asked, "How so?"

"We can talk about that later. You said that after Mogadishu, everything changed with the anger problems," said Dorne. "I'm waiting to hear what changed."

Josh shrugged and said, "It's hard to explain. I felt calm and alive during that battle. My two buddies who were along with the group had to be chaptered out of the Army because the experience drove them batty. But I liked it. Everything moved in slow motion. I was serene."

"Did the killing and death affect you?" Asked Dorne.

"Not at all," Josh said, "In fact, I rarely think about it."

"Mm-hm," muttered Dorne. "So what changed?"

"After my experience in Mogadishu, everything seemed so trivial," Josh said. "Every order seemed trivial. Every non-combat related training event seemed trivial. The anger became worse because nothing mattered. Officers and superiors bitching was and is utter bullshit. Since then, my tolerance for bullshit has bottomed out. Biting my tongue until it bleeds seems to help. So does flexing my calves until they cramp."

"So why did you leave the Rangers?" Asked Dorne.

"After Somalia, I knew I'd lose my mind at the Ranger Regiment," Josh said, "so I applied for Delta selection. I didn't make it past the first psych eval. Apparently, they thought I was damaged goods. After being kicked out of selection, I found out about this Counterintelligence program. It sounded cool at the time, so I re-enlisted and transferred to the MI branch. And here I am."

Dorne opened the laptop again and surveyed the screen for a moment. Without looking up from the screen, he asked, "Do *you* think you're damaged goods?"

Josh didn't hesitate; " I know my weaknesses and I do my best to keep them under control, but sometimes they bubble over. That's what you saw this morning."

"How often have you been in trouble throughout your career? How many Article 15's have you received?" asked Dorne, still staring at the screen.

"None until I got to this unit," said Josh. He thought for a moment, then added, "I've received three thus far, and I have at least three more on deck. I guess I'm just getting sloppy."

"I doubt that," Dorne shut the laptop. "What you're gonna want to do is take exit 43, take a right at the first light, loop around left, then find a good bumper location off the traffic circle across from the La Roseraie. We'll watch the entrance. Exit 43 should be coming up in about 15 clicks. You married?"

"Nope," replied Josh.

"Ever been married?"

Josh smiled and replied, "Nope."

"You gay?"

Josh looked at Dorne. He was studying a diagram and some photographs. "Uh, I don't think you're allowed to ask that, Dorne, and I'm not obligated to tell."

"I'm sure as hell not military, Joshua. You gay?"

Josh shook his head and smirked, "Nope."

"Mm-hm." Dorne opened the laptop again and pecked at the keyboard. "Step on it, Joshua. I want us to be set for the comms check in 15 minutes."

1045 HOURS, 24 OCTOBER 1998 – LA ROSERAIE HOTEL, BRUSSELS, BELGIUM

There wasn't much more he could do at this point. Kolya had spent the better part of an hour trying to figure out how to get rid of the bodies. He couldn't just carry them to the trash bin behind the hotel. It was too light outside, even with the heavy clouds and mist. Kolya wished for a moment that Vyatcheslav hadn't killed Oleg back in Vidnoye. Oleg would've known what to do.

Kolya settled on stuffing the bodies under the bed. He had called the front desk and requested another night and no maid service. That would give enough time to make the delivery and get out of Europe altogether.

He'd spent the last hour sitting on a chair across from the Halliburton case and fantasizing about the ten percent cut he'd get the moment he delivered the case to the customers. Eight hours, four stops, and a delivery. He'd be out of the business in only eight hours!

Kolya deserved retirement, after all. He'd worked for Dmitriy since 1991, and his jobs were most unpleasant. Establishing smuggling routes, killing or intimidating competitors, and being a courier for important or dangerous things like this case. And since Dmitriy had started working with the American, the jobs were becoming more frequent and more brutal. Some of the American's jobs and methods didn't make any sense. Like this one--why entrust something so important to someone like Kolya? And why must Kolya go alone today? Kolya rubbed his right forearm as he pondered these questions.

Oleg would know the answers, he thought. Instead of thinking too hard, which usually made his head hurt, he went back to staring at the case and fantasizing about retirement. When he looked up at the clock after a few minutes, it read 1057.

27

"Dermo nah vashem litseh!" Kolya grabbed his own full bag in one hand and gathered the Halliburton case in the other just after he opened the door. Muttering curses, he jogged to the black Mercedes. He slipped on the wet pavement right behind the vehicle and dropped the Halliburton case.

"Yeb t'voy maht!" he muttered over and over as he gathered himself, picked up the case, loaded it in the trunk and made his way to the driver's side door.

1100 HOURS, 24 OCTOBER 1998 – LA ROSERAIE HOTEL, BRUSSELS, BELGIUM

All five vehicles had been in place for an hour, each covering a different possible target vehicle egress. The calls began coming at exactly 1057 hours.

Surveillance had always been a thing of beauty for Josh. It was less of a science and more of an art. Every time that initial call came out over the radio, Josh felt a rush of adrenaline. This time was no different.

"7777! That's Charlie. Zulu 1 is no longer complete the hotel. Zulu 1 is 91 the cup of the hotel. Wait. Zulus 2 and 3 unsighted. Zulu 1 is intending complete X-ray 1. Wait."

A good surveillant didn't hear the codes. Josh heard:

"Attention everyone! This is the third vehicle on the team, and we can see Kolya Aliyev. Kolya Aliyev has exited his hotel room. Kolya Aliyev is heading toward the hotel parking lot. No sign of his two thugs. Kolya Aliyev is preparing to enter the black Mercedes. Wait."

Since Joshua was in the Sierra Charlie vehicle, he responded; "Alpha," which meant, 'Acknowledged.'

"Third vehicle. Kolya Aliyev slipped in the parking lot near the Mercedes and dropped a metal case. Wait."

Dorne hissed through his teeth when he heard the call.

"Acknowledged," Josh responded.

"Third vehicle. Kolya Aliyev is back up and getting in his vehicle. Still no sign of the two thugs, wait."

"Acknowledged."

"Hmm," Dorne muttered. "This is already starting all wrong."

"Third vehicle. Kolya Aliyev has entered the black Mercedes, license plate number BH 145 989, has started it, and is moving toward the exit."

Dorne grabbed the hand mic from Josh and said, "Third vehicle, stay in place and await instructions. Fourth vehicle, take the black Mercedes out. Remember everyone, no need to stay too far back on this one. Make sure you have him at all times."

The third vehicle acknowledged and the fourth followed the Mercedes. Josh ran through each vehicle occupant in his mind. It appeared Chief Smith and Staff Sergeant Tyler in the third vehicle would be staying to search Kolya Aliyev's room, and determine what happened to the two thugs.

Kolya took the same road out that the team had taken in. He got on the E19 and headed East. Josh and Dorne took up the rear and monitored the follow. Dorne threw the curtain aside and went to the back of the van. He came back into the cab a few minutes later and called Smith and Tyler via cell phone.

"Hey Smith. Dorne. The two thugs checked out about 45 minutes before we arrived. It seems Kolya extended his stay. Go ahead and search his room. I've arranged for a key to be waiting for you at the front desk. No. No. No. No!" Dorne was getting flustered at whatever Chief Smith was asking him. "I don't give a shit if he knows you were in there! Just follow instructions, Chief. Out."

"What it is with these warrant officers?" Dorne asked rhetorically. He grabbed the hand mic from Josh. "All vehicles. Make sure you stay close on Aliyev. I say again: Stay close!"

All the vehicles acknowledged. Dorne sighed and opened the laptop again. When Aliyev got off the E19 and onto the E40, Dorne observed; "He's heading to Maastricht."

Dorne again went to the back of the van. Josh could hear him pecking at keys. Josh went out on a limb and asked over his shoulder, "Why Maastricht?"

Dorne answered from the back, "That's where his coke hook-up is in Holland. I think he's going to pick up some drugs and maybe a weapon. This guy can't go more than a couple hours without a spike, and I don't think he's armed. He's going to want to be armed."

"You think he's going to make some kind of weapons deal there?" asked Josh. Again, Josh knew he was pressing his luck. This operation was thin on details, and Dorne likely wanted it that way.

"No," Dorne answered. "If he's going to sell what's in the case, it'll probably be in Germany. I guess we'll see. When he stops in Maastricht, we'll stay on the vehicle."

"Do you want me to relay some of these details to the team?" asked Josh.

"No," Dorne answered.

"Why not?"

Dorne tossed the curtain aside, looked at Josh through the rear view mirror and said; "Because I have a feeling this is your lucky day, Joshua."

1215 hours, 24 October 1998 – Maastricht, The Netherlands

Kolya pulled into the parking structure, found a spot on the fifth level, parked and waited. When he was sure no one had followed him to the fifth level, he turned the car off and popped the trunk. He collected the Halliburton case and made his way to the elevator.

He'd seen two vehicles following a little too close on the E40. He might be under surveillance, but he might not. He'd only made two turns until he got to Maastricht, and on his way into downtown, he hadn't noticed any vehicles following him.

As he descended to the basement level, his head started to pound. It had been at least 8 hours since he'd spiked, and he needed a fix. He also needed a weapon. If he was being followed, he couldn't take any chances. He'd have to call the American, as well.

When the elevator doors opened to the basement, Kolya took an immediate left out of the elevator and made his way down a narrow hallway. It reeked of Indian food. Always did down here. He arrived at a wooden door at the end of the hall. Next to the door was a pile of leaky garbage bags. The scent of rotting chicken flesh and curry was overpowering. He stepped around the pile and pounded on the door five times.

A gaunt Indian man opened the door and stepped aside when he recognized Kolya.

"Is he upstairs?" asked Kolya as he shoved past the Indian man.

"Ja," the skinny Indian replied.

Kolya walked through the kitchen to the staircase. He lumbered up the stairs, through the semi-crowded restaurant and into the office at the back. When he opened the door, a fat Dutchman stood up from the desk in the rear of the room.

"My friend!" the man said as he waddled toward Kolya with his arms spread wide.

"No hug, Joren," Kolya said, "I need fix, and I need to use phone."

Joren stopped short of Kolya and said, "Of course, of course. My friend, why have you not been around? It has been too long." He made his way around to his desk and plopped down. He opened a bottom drawer and pulled out a small zip-top baggy with at least 20 grams of cocaine. He tossed it to Kolya.

Kolya caught the bag and nodded thanks at Joren. He pulled a chair to the desk, sat down and placed the Halliburton case next to the chair.

Joren leaned across the stained surface and looked at the case. "You have come to sell me something nice?"

"You cannot afford," replied Kolya. He pulled a thick roll of Dutch gilders out of his jacket and tossed it to Joren. "Is enough?"

Joren fumbled the catch. He leaned over to retrieve the roll. When he picked it up and examined the roll, he said, "This is far too much, Kolya. You want more cocaine than what I gave you there?"

"No," Kolya answered, "I need pistol and rifle, also."

"Of course, of course," Joren said. He swiveled his chair around and punched a code into a wall safe. He opened the door and moved aside. "Which would you like?"

Kolya glanced in the safe and said, "The Kalash and the Beretta. Need bullets." Kolya reached over the desk and grabbed the phone as Joren pulled the AK-47 and the Beretta 9mm out of the safe. Kolya dialed the 20 digit number and waited for the call to be routed.

When the line connected, the American immediately answered and yelled, "What the fuck are you doing in Maastricht?!"

"Why you know I am at Maastricht?" asked Kolya.

"Moron: Look at your *arm*!" the American raged, "How many times do we have to do this? You're obviously intent on not following instructions. What is the problem?"

"Maybe I am followed," Kolya said as he rubbed his forearm.

"'Maybe'? 'Maybe'? Damn it, Kolya, there is no maybe. How many vehicles have you seen?"

"Two."

"And was it over time, distance and direction?" asked the American.

Kolya was puzzled. He didn't understand this spy game nonsense. He didn't know how to respond, so he just replied, "Yes."

"How could you let this happen?! Why did you deviate?!" screamed the American. After a moment, the American spoke again, calmly and in Russian; "Listen, Kolya. You remember Akescht?"

"Da," Kolya answered. "Luxembourg."

"Go to Akescht. I'll arrange for the exchange to take place there," said the American. "And Kolya..."

"Da."

"No more deviations." The American hung up.

1250 hours, 24 October 1998 – Maastricht, The Netherlands

"He's been in there 30 minutes. You sure you don't want me to go in?" asked Josh. "I'm wired up."

"I'm sure," replied Dorne from the back of the van. "You wouldn't fit in with that sorry excuse for business attire."

"What should I tell the team?" asked Josh. The remaining four vehicles had been calling for status updates every two minutes.

"Tell them to hold!" yelled Dorne. "You're the Sierra Charlie. Get your team under control!"

Just then, the cell phone rang.

"Hand it to me," Dorne said.

Josh picked up the phone and moved the curtain aside to hand it back. Dorne snatched the phone from Joshua's hand and put it up to his own ear. Josh listened to Dorne's end of the conversation.

"What? Repeat that. You did *what*? And you're *just now* telling me?! Absolutely not...... No, *this* remains the priority...... Chief Smith, I am going to say this once. Just once: You will not call off this surveillance... I don't give a damn! Well, lucky for us we're in The Netherlands... Don't you do it... Don't you hang up... Shit!"

The phone flew through the curtain and crashed against the windshield. Then there was a calm silence in the back of the van. Josh didn't dare speak first. Obviously plans had changed.

A call finally came through on the radio and broke the silence; "That's Bravo, returning to base."

Immediately another call; "That's Delta, returning to base."

Then finally; "That's Echo, returning to base."

Josh simply responded, "Acknowledged."

After a few more moments of silence, Josh heard a frenzy of activity in the back of the van: furious pecking keyboards, turning dials and the hum of hard drives and fans.

Every two minutes, Dorne would say; "Make sure you watch that exit. It's the only one."

Josh didn't take his eyes off the parking structure exit, but his mind was reeling. What the hell was going on?

When the black Mercedes pulled out of the garage and onto Vaasstraat, Josh took the binoculars and verified the plate. "He's out. Heading east on Vaasstraat."

"Well follow him, Joshua."

Josh put the van into gear and pulled out about 600 feet behind the black Mercedes. "Do we know it's Aliyev?"

"Doesn't matter," Dorne said from the back. He was still typing away. "Keep following him. No need to stay too far back."

Josh could hear Dorne pressing keys on what had to be a satellite phone. There was a slight pause, then Dorne began speaking. Josh didn't speak or comprehend Dutch, but he recognized the language. Dorne spoke for about two minutes, then dialed another number. This time, he spoke German. After that, Dorne made another call, this time speaking French.

When Dorne emerged from the back of the van and sat down, Josh had followed the Mercedes out of downtown Maastricht and onto the A76 heading northeast toward Cologne, Germany. Just as Dorne got settled and pulled his seatbelt across his shoulder, Josh's personal cell phone rang.

"Don't answer it," Dorne said as he clicked his seatbelt.

Josh glanced at his phone sitting in the console. It was Beebe's office number calling. "You're putting me in a tight spot, Dorne."

"I know it, buddy," Dorne said, "but I need you here more than they need you there."

"I don't think an explanation is too much to ask," Josh said.

"Fair enough," Dorne opened the laptop again and turned the screen toward Josh. "Without running us off the highway, take a look at this. You see that blue dot on up there? That's your buddy Chief Smith back at La Roseraie. Those three blue dots further south are your buddies heading back to La Roseraie. That blue dot there is us, and the yellow dot in front of us....the yellow dot is that silver case. Inside that silver case is between 6 and 10 kilograms of refined plutonium-239."

Josh swerved into the left lane. A high pitched honk brought his attention back to the road.

"Do I have your attention now?" asked Dorne as he slapped the laptop closed.

"Why did they go back?"

"When Smith and Tyler were searching the room, they found two dead women. Hookers, probably. That's Kolya's M.O. Instead of calling me, those imbeciles called the Belgian police. When the police showed up, they detained Smith and Tyler for questioning and ordered them to recall the team. Smith complied and called off the surveillance. Joshua, we can't let him just drive away. We have to see where he's going."

Josh eased back from the Mercedes a few car lengths. "Man, I'm going to be in big trouble."

"I know," said Dorne, "but do you care?"

"In this case, no," Josh answered, "but I'm confused. Why don't we call in some support?"

"I have," Dorne answered.

"More call signs? From where?"

"I called in support," Dorne said.

"That's pretty vague. Who are you?"

"Does it matter?" Dorne returned.

Josh thought for a moment. In the end, it really didn't matter who Dorne's employer might be. Josh settled on the conclusion that Dorne worked for the US Government in some capacity, and all that mattered was that metal case and its contents. Josh didn't know why he believed Dorne. Someone placed him in charge of this mission. He had to be *somebody*. He finally answered Dorne's question with a definitive 'no', but he asked a question in return; "Is this still my lucky day?"

Dorne just smiled.

1435 HOURS, 24 OCTOBER 1998 – A76 AUTOBAHN, OUTSKIRTS OF COLOGNE, GERMANY

Kolya had finally found a radio station playing Norwegian death metal. He hadn't seen either of the two cars he had spotted behind him on the way to Maastricht. In celebration, he had already snorted about eight ounces of cocaine. Good stuff Joren, he thought. He'd been speeding out so hard he'd forgotten he had to piss, but the sharp pressure just below his belt finally broke through the high.

He pulled over at the first rest stop he saw. He decided to forgo the public restroom experience and elected to urinate on the ground behind the Mercedes. He finished, zipped his fly and got back into the Mercedes. He chopped up one more line, snorted it and cranked the metal.

This could very well be the highest I've ever been, thought Kolya. It's fine, though. This is a celebration. Only a few hours from retirement. Drop the case in Akescht and off I go, he mused.

Instead of the scheduled stop in Cologne, he'd take a shortcut. What difference did it make? The sooner he got this done, the better.

"Amerikansi. Yeb t'voy maht," he muttered through the ear-splitting metal as he veered onto the A1 and headed south toward Prum, Germany. He wiped his nose and didn't notice the blood, nor did he notice his hands were shaking like a Parkinson's victim.

1445 HOURS, 24 OCTOBER 1998 – A1 AUTOBAHN, OUTSKIRTS OF COLOGNE, GERMANY

"How in the hell did he not see us? We drove right by him! When he was pissing, he was looking right at us!"

"He's flying high," Dorne said. "Didn't you see him shaking? I'd say he's about five grams away from an overdose. At least we know for a fact it's him driving the Mercedes."

"What if he passes out and wrecks? Is that plutonium going to contaminate anything?" asked Josh as he watched Aliyev pass them and merge back the A1.

"Naw," said Dorne, "It's probably stable. No real risk unless it's a ball, and I doubt it's a ball."

"So why did you hiss when he dropped the case back at La Roseraie?"

"You never know, Joshua. It's plutonium."

"Great," Josh said. He eased the van onto the A1 and fell in about a quarter of a mile behind Kolya. Dorne hadn't closed his laptop in the last 30 minutes. Josh noticed he had other programs running in addition to the mapping program. Josh thought about the blue dots and the trouble he was in at the moment. He shuddered at the thought of Beebe's imminent haranguing. He started to reason through the situation, and decided Dorne owed him a little more information.

"Dorne, I'm helping you out here because it's the right thing to do. But I have to ask for some top cover."

"About time you asked," Dorne said, switching through programs on the laptop. "I arranged for a call to be made to your unit informing them I have returned to base, and you would make your way back to Belgium via train. So we have a few hours, here."

Josh was still confused. This wasn't normal. Intelligence was a shadowy and mysterious field with all the different agencies and their missions, but this was odd. Why this level of deception? Had Dorne thrown this mission together at the last minute? Were his superiors aware of his activities? For the second time, Josh realized he didn't really care.

"Must be nice," Josh said.

"What?"

"This level of freedom to conduct your operations."

"It is nice," Dorne said, "I get a lot done this way, and that is a fact. What would happen if we let this guy go when Smith called off the surveillance?"

"Yeah," Josh said in support of Dorne's point.

"No, I'm asking you to tell me what you think would happen." Dorne said.

"Well," Josh began, "I suppose we'd inform our partner nations' intelligence services."

"Yes, that's what you'd do. You'd call up the Belgians, the Dutch, and now the Germans to let them know between 6 and 10 kilograms of refined plutonium 239 is loose in their countries. Then what would happen? I'll tell you what would happen because I've seen it: All Hell would break loose. They'd spend the better half of a day concocting their response. By that time, this particular case would be long gone. Then the inevitable damage control would be the flavor of the week. They'd have to find someone to blame, and at the end of it all; you, Joshua Quinn, would still be in hot water--you know I'm right. They'd find a way to blame the low man."

Josh nodded unconsciously. This was all eerily making sense.

Dorne went on; "But we're getting ahead of ourselves here. Everything I just said is based on the premise that anyone even knew Aliyev was carrying plutonium. So let's take that off the table and leave it at this: If I wasn't here taking care of this, enough plutonium to construct a 20 megaton nuclear weapon would be sold to God knows who. I'm going to tell you the truest thing you'll ever hear: most, if not all intelligence agencies on this planet couldn't find snow in winter. Any successes they enjoy are blind luck these days. I could go on and on, but by the look on your face I don't need to do that. You know I'm right. Look how many collection platforms we had in Somalia, and look how it all turned out."

"You're part of that system," Josh said.

"Am I?" Dorne asked. "Hey, you're getting a little too far back. Looks like he's picked up the pace."

"Do you know where he's headed?"

"Thought I did until Maastricht," Dorne said. "Something altered his plans. Kolya's always been a bit unhinged. What's amazing to me is that he isn't acting like he's under surveillance."

This wasn't adding up for Josh. Deliberate preventative surveillance on a guy who had plutonium? Dorne had basically contracted a bunch of unknown quantities to participate in this surveillance, and to what end? Josh voiced his questions. Dorne looked up at the wet road ahead and seemed to be contemplating a reply, but he simply said, "It's complicated," and turned his attention back to the laptop.

After a few minutes, Dorne got up and went to the back of the van again. This time, Josh heard him chambering rounds. "Just in case!" he yelled cheerfully from the back.

1630 HOURS, 24 OCTOBER 1998 – B51 AUTOBAHN, PRUM, GERMANY

Germany in October, Josh thought as he flipped on the headlights and the windshield wipers. Was that sleet? God forbid he'd have to run on slippery pavement in these cheap loafers.

Other than the occasional status updates, Josh and Dorne hadn't spoken much over the last two hours. Dorne had been in the back fussing with whatever equipment he had stashed back there. Josh had been chewing on the non sequiturs of this situation. He'd turned his personal cell phone off after the fifteenth missed call from Beebe. Despite the fact he was involved in an operation that had direct national security implications, he was depressed. When this was all over, he'd have to go back to his unit. He'd have to deal with the same ass reamings, Article 15's and botched operations. Here I am literally saving the world, he thought, and I'm going to get shredded for it. All he'd ever wanted to do in the military was make a difference, and he felt empty despite the fact he was doing something spectacularly crucial for national security at this very moment. You're feeling sorry for yourself, thought Josh, this is what you signed up for. This whole thing isn't anyone's fault but your own. He'd be damned, though, if he would show the least amount of remorse for disobeying the order to cease the surveillance. He'd gladly pay the price for that insubordination.

Lost in thoughts of standing up to Beebe, he nearly missed Kolya's abrupt lane change to veer off the B51 and onto the B410 to Luxembourg. Fortunately, Josh had plenty of time to make the exit without swerving.

Josh leaned his head toward the curtain; "Dorne."

"Yeah."

"He's on the B410 to Luxembourg. If memory serves, he'll only be in Germany another twenty minutes if he stays on this autobahn."

42

"Yeah."

Josh heard something that sounded like a heavy stomp on the van floor. He didn't know if Dorne didn't understand exactly what he was telling him. As a reminder Josh said, "I don't remember Luxembourg on the list of countries we can enter."

Another thud that sounded like a shoe hitting the van floor.

"Joshua, haven't you figured out I don't give a shit about something as insignificant as a border?"

1730 HOURS, 24 OCTOBER 1998 – B50 AUTOBAHN, LUXEMBOURG / GERMANY BORDER

Rheinland-Phalz on the left and Luxembourg on the right. When Aliyev took the exit to enter Luxembourg, Josh followed without hesitation knowing things would never be the same if this follow went sour in any way. Hell, even if it went fine, things wouldn't be the same. But what would make it sour or fine? He knew Dorne wasn't going to let that case go anywhere outside his control. The way Dorne carried himself, Josh could see he had control of the Halliburton case since the beginning of the follow. He wasn't going to let it go. Josh knew this would boil down to some sort of confrontation; there was no way around it.

Dorne was still in the back, flitting around and not speaking. Josh would give him regular updates, but Dorne would only grunt 'yeah' or an 'mm-hm'.

The B50 began to make the transition from autobahn freeway to a country highway, winding through the slightly hilly Luxembourg landscape. Ten kilometers further in, the B50 turned from a country highway to a winding country road; barely two lanes.

"Okay," Dorne said from the rear, "start backing off a bit."

When Kolya topped the hill ahead of them, Josh tapped the breaks to increase the distance between vehicles a solid half kilometer. When Josh crested the hill, he could barely see Kolya's tail lights through the sleet.

"Good," Dorne said from the back, "That'll do." It was as if he was watching. Josh turned his head to make sure Dorne wasn't peeking through the curtain. He wasn't.

"I won't be able to see him if he turns off around a bend or over a hill," Josh said.

"There aren't many turn offs," Dorne said, "Plus I think I know where he's going."

They wound through the Luxembourg countryside for a few more kilometers, passing the occasional dimly lit farmhouse. The sleet had turned to a light snow, making the drive a bit more treacherous. Josh could handle a car just fine, but a high center of gravity van was a different story. On some of the winding turns, the rear end of the van began to slide a bit. Through the light snow, Josh could make out the outline of a small hill on the horizon.

"Alright," Dorne said as he swished the curtain aside and climbed back into the passenger seat. Josh saw Dorne had changed out of his $500 leather shoes and into black combat boots. Joshua raised an eyebrow that although the footwear had changed, the Dorne was still wearing the expensive suit. "See that hill about a kilometer ahead? The road winds around the base of the hill. When you get to the base, you'll see a turnoff to the right. Turn off there and park it."

When they reached the turnoff, Josh pulled the van over. It slid to a stop in the light dusting of snow. Dorne opened the laptop and looked at the screen for a few moments.

"Here we go," he said, "You ready?"

Josh nodded his head yes. Ready for what? he wondered.

"Alright," Dorne began, "Here's the deal: he's headed to a farmhouse about 500 meters from this spot. It's on the other side of this hill. You and I are proceeding on foot over the hill and coming up on the back side of the farmhouse. We're going to get that case. I'll take care of everything, I just need you to provide over-watch from the tree line behind the farmhouse. When I come out of the house with the case, if anyone is following me, take them out."

Dorne didn't wait for questions. He opened the door and went around to the back of the van. Josh followed his lead. When Josh got to the back of the van, Dorne already had both doors open. The rear of the vehicle was full of electronic equipment. Computer monitors, spectrometers, a single work station, and a small locker in the right rear corner. Dorne was rummaging through the locker. He pulled out a black tactical vest and put it on over his suit coat. Attached to the vest were full magazine ouches, flash-bang grenades, flares, a Bowie knife, and an assortment of small pockets. When he zipped the front, he reached back into the locker, retrieved another vest and gave it to Josh. As Josh donned the vest, Dorne stared at Josh's feet.

"What size do you wear?" he asked.

"12," Josh answered.

"I guess squeezing into 10 ½ is out of the question," Dorne said, "It's going to be rough going with those loafers. How much did you pay for those?"

"Forty bucks," Josh answered as he zipped up his vest.

"Worth every penny," Dorne quipped. He reached back in the locker and pulled out a short pump shotgun with no stock. He clipped it to the side of his vest and reached back in the locker. He pulled out an M4 carbine with optics and slung it over his body.

"All I have is two M4s. You okay with that?" Dorne asked as he handed Josh one carbine.

Josh took the M4 and examined the optic. He'd never used optics before, and he wasn't sure how much good it would do in the dark. He was about to ask Dorne about taking off the optic when Dorne handed him a pair of what looked to be 'terminator' sunglasses senior citizens often wear. Josh put them on and looked out toward the base of the hill. He staggered in surprise.

The Night Vision Goggles he had used in the past were cumbersome and too one-dimensional. This device was different. Everything seen through these glasses had three-dimensional shape and depth. Where the old NVGs showed everything in a greenish hue, these 'terminators' displayed everything in full color. Josh pulled them off and examined them with surprise.

Dorne saw his fascination and commented, "Pretty cool, huh? They're compatible with the optic, too."

Josh put them on his face again and said, "Where did you...never-mind."

Dorne chuckled and shut the van doors. He and Josh went over the plan again. When they finished checking their weapons and gear one last time, they set out at a jog up the hill.

1815 HOURS, 24 OCTOBER 1998 – AKESCHT, LUXEMBOURG

Kolya had a bad feeling when he first saw the farmhouse. No lights. No tire tracks in the light dusting of snow. As he neared the plain stone and wood building, he turned on his high beams. No vehicles. He pulled up to the house and tried to make a loop around the front yard. The mud was too thick in spots and his front tires were losing traction. He stopped and put the Mercedes in reverse. The rear tires spun and couldn't find any traction at all. He shifted it into drive and floored it. He could feel the front end sinking in the mud. He screamed curses and slammed the steering wheel with his fists and palms until it was bent ninety degrees and pinned against the steering column. He took out the satellite phone and tried to call the American. No answer. He tried again. No connection. He tried yet again. This time the phone wouldn't even pick up any satellites.

Kolya's mind reeled on the edge of panic. He knew this was the right place: the farmhouse in Akescht. He'd been here many times to exchange drugs, arms or women for money. The American had said Akescht. The American was precise and never mistaken. Why send him to an abandoned house with $36 million worth of merchandise? Oleg would know what to do. What would Oleg say? Oleg would say the buyers weren't here yet. He should go inside and wait for the buyers, but he should go armed and be ready for anything. And when the buyers showed up, he could almost hear Oleg's voice, charge them an extra five percent for making him wait.

Oleg collected the remaining cocaine, his AK and the Beretta, the case and his own bag. He then trudged toward the house, occasionally slipping in the mud and yelling curses. He kicked in the front door, entered the decrepit house and slammed the door behind him.

1830 HOURS, 24 OCTOBER 1998 – AKESCHT, LUXEMBOURG

"What's he yelling about?" Josh whispered.

Dorne surveyed the front yard of the farmhouse for a moment, then whispered back; "Looks like he got his Mercedes stuck in the mud over there. He's also probably pissed no one is here to receive him."

They had taken a position in the tree line caddy corner to the back of the farmhouse. From here they could observe the back and front of the old structure. They hadn't arrived in time to see Aliyev pull up to the house because of Josh's slipping and sliding up and down the hill.

He and Josh remained in place for another 15 minutes. The snow had stopped and the skies cleared, dropping the temperature about 10 degrees. Josh's fingers, toes and ears were numb and beginning to ache. He also realized he hadn't eaten in about 24 hours. Dorne remained silent. He was stroking his chin over and over, obviously trying to decide what to do.

"Hand me the laptop," he whispered.

Josh took the laptop out of a pouch on the side of his vest and handed it to Dorne. Dorne unzipped his vest, laid it aside and then took off his suit jacket. He draped it over the laptop, turned the computer on and put his head under the makeshift shroud. He pecked at a few keys then slapped the laptop closed.

"Shit!" he hissed as he threw off the suit coat and scrambled to put his vest back on.

"What is it?" Josh whispered.

Dorne raised his voice to a normal, not worried about whispering; "Listen to me very carefully. I'm going in there," he motioned at the farmhouse, "and when I'm done, I'm going to toss a blue flare out the window. When you see that blue flare, you run like your life depends on it back to the van." He unhooked the shotgun from his vest and pumped the shells out onto the ground. He reached into one of the pockets on his vest and withdrew four green shotgun shells labeled 'less than lethal', and fed them into the shotgun. "When you get there," he continued, "reach under the passenger side dash. You'll feel a lever. Twist it clockwise and run back to the tree line at the base of the hill and wait. When it's clear, make your way back to Belgium. I'll find you and make all this right." He grabbed Josh's vest and yanked it; "You got me?"

"Yeah," Josh said. "What if I don't see the blue flare?"

"Then you go in there and kill that son of a bitch," answered Dorne. "But you'll see the flare. I promise you that much. You just cover the rear. If he comes out, shoot him low. You figure out the rest, *Ranger*." He slapped Josh on the back and ran through the swirling snow toward the back of the farmhouse.

1905 HOURS, 24 OCTOBER 1998 – AKESCHT, LUXEMBOURG

It happened faster than Josh thought possible. When Dorne reached the back porch, he threw a flash bang grenade through a window and backed against the door. As soon as Josh felt the concussion, Dorne threw another through the broken window. Dorne repeated this three more times, then kicked the door and charged inside. Josh heard three shotgun blasts in rapid succession, then another window shattered and a blue flare landed ten feet off the back porch.

"Go!" he heard Dorne scream from inside the house. Josh took off at a full sprint up the hill toward the van on the other side. He had taken off his loafers and socks to give him a little more traction for the 500 meter run.

He made it to the van in just over three minutes. His lungs were burning from huffing in the ice cold air. He couldn't feel his feet anymore, but he must have turned his ankle on the run because he was limping when he made his way around to the passenger side. As he was unlocking the door, he saw three sets of headlights coming down the road toward the van. Josh fumbled the keys with his numb fingers, but he finally got the door open. He glanced at the headlights. They were right on him. As he reached under the dash, he heard the vehicles coming to a screeching halt just behind the van. Finally, his hand found the lever. He twisted it clockwise, and it wouldn't budge.

"Get out of the van!" Someone yelled from behind. "Get out of the van and get on the ground!"

Josh put all his weight into the lever. It finally gave and twisted 45 degrees clockwise. Josh heard a hissing sound from the back of the van as he turned to run. He took four or five bounding steps before three shots were fired over his head. He dropped to the ground spread eagle with his hands behind his neck.

"He's armed!" someone yelled. The hissing sound became louder and the air began to smell of burning electronics. Someone else yelled, "It's on fire!"

A meaty hand grabbed the back of Josh's vest and dragged him thirty feet away from the van. A knee dug into the back of his neck, burying his face in the snow and mud and crushing his nose and the 'terminators'. His pistol was gruffly unholstered and his rifle unslung. He could feel and hear the vest being cut off his body.

"Now get up, and get on your knees with your hands interlocked behind your head," someone ordered.

Josh complied and pulled himself up. He could feel the heat from the van which, from the sound of it, was a giant fireball now. A bright light shined in his face.

"It's not him," someone said. It finally occurred to Joshua that the men were speaking English. American English.

A door slam. Josh turned his head toward the sound and got a glimpse of the vehicles. Three dark Suburbans. There were five men decked out in black tactical gear surrounding Josh with MP5s trained on him. A man in a suit like Dorne's but with a garish green tie was walking toward Josh from one of the Suburbans. He shouldered past the men in black and grabbed Josh by the lapels and forced him to his feet.

"Who the fuck are you?!" the man in the tie yelled, "and where the fuck is *he*?!"

Josh was beyond confused. He had entered a state of shock. "Who?"

The man backhanded Josh so hard he fell to the ground. He kicked Josh in the gut, grabbed him roughly and forced him back up. "Don't be a smart ass! You're in way over your head! Where is the person who owns this van?!"

Josh motioned over the hill. The man in the green tie let go of Josh's coat and shoved him back. Josh tripped over his vest and landed butt first in the mud. Someone kicked him on the chest and rolled him over. A knee landed on his neck again. Josh could taste blood in the back of his throat.

"Alpha and Bravo," the man said, "let's get to that farmhouse. Charlie, try to put out that fire, and try to salvage anything from that van. Identify that piece of shit and keep him on the ground until we get back."

Josh heard footsteps going toward the Suburbans, then the scratching of tires peeling out of the turnoff and toward the farmhouse. Hands were going over his body, searching.

"Back pocket," Josh said. The knee mashed against his neck harder as the hands went to his back pocket and pulled out his badge and credentials, then his wallet.

"Special Agent Joshua D. Quinn?"

"Yes. That's me," Josh strained. He could barely breathe through the blood and snow and mud.

"Get him to his knees," someone said.

One man hauled Josh to his knees and ordered him to interlock his hands behind his head. Josh looked around and saw only three men. One was walking from the remaining Suburban toward the van with a small fire extinguisher in hand. Josh could still feel the heat from the burning van. He's not going to get that fire out, thought Josh.

Neither of the men guarding him said anything more. They simply stood there with their MP5s trained on him while the third tried in vain to extinguish the flaming van. The tires began to blow, but the men didn't flinch. After about thirty seconds, the small extinguisher was spent. The third man cursed and threw it into the conflagration. He turned and walked back to the two men guarding Josh. He picked up the 'terminators' and examined them. He handed the NVGs and Josh's vest to one of the other men without saying a word.

After two speechless minutes passed, Josh could hear the sound of automatic gunfire from the farmhouse. First he heard the repeat of MP5 fire, the answering carbine fire. Dorne was in a firefight with these men. Josh counted four exchanges of MP5 and M4 fire, then about a minute of silence. He heard three concussions which must have been flash-bang grenades, then more M4 fire. By Josh's count, Dorne was probably on his third magazine.

After a few more exchanges, Josh picked up a faint sound he hadn't heard since October 1993. It was a low whine coming from the south, following the same path Josh and Dorne had come in. The whine grew louder as it quickly approached. It suddenly appeared out of the snowy dimness, buzzing overhead about thirty feet and stirring up snow. It fanned the flames from the van toward Josh and the men as it passed. An AH-6 Little Bird. Josh caught its outline when it buzzed the turnoff and swept up and over the hill. It had a bench on one side and what looked to be a 7.62mm mini-gun on the other.

As soon as the Little Bird disappeared over the hill, Josh's observation of the mini-gun was confirmed by the buzz. The Little Bird was firing on something near the farmhouse. The three men were giving one another questioning looks, and one of them dashed back to the Suburban. He opened the driver side door, pulled out a hand mike and began making frantic queries. The Little Bird obviously wasn't theirs. Of the countless possible questions, one dominated Josh's thoughts: Who in the hell is Bradley Dorne?

2003 HOURS, 24 OCTOBER 1998 – AKESCHT, LUXEMBOURG

It had been at least half an hour since the Little Bird had left the scene and flown north. It had stayed on station at the farmhouse for about five minutes and flown away. Josh was still on his knees with his hands behind his head when the two Suburbans came back up the road and parked near the third. One of them was full of holes on the passenger side, and the other's bullet resistant windows were hit so many times on the passenger side, they were an opaque white of shattered fiberglass.

Josh's legs were in knots, his nose felt broken and his hands were now completely numb. He knew his feet were frostbitten at this point. He wondered if he'd lose any of his toes.

The same man in the expensive suit and green tie got out of the Suburban with the shot up windows and walked toward Josh. He had something wrapped in plastic in his hands, and he brandished it as if he was going to beat Josh with it. As he neared, Josh could see the plastic was bloody on one end. The man in the tie took the thing by one end and let it fall out of the wrapping in front of Josh. It hit Josh's lower legs and rolled directly in front of him. It was the lower half of a man's right arm, cut off just below the elbow. Whoever had severed the arm wasn't surgical about it. It looked like it had been mangled off with a butter knife. Josh looked up at the man, puzzled. The man backhanded him again.

"I know you're in over your head, but what do you know about this?" the man in the tie asked as Josh made his way back to his knees.

"I'm Special Agent Joshua Quinn, US Army Intelligence," Josh began. He thought he'd try to explain himself. These guys were obviously Americans, after all. There had to be some kind of misunderstanding here.

"I don't give a fuck what your name is," the man spat and motioned to the blazing van, "tell me what you know about the man who owned that."

"Bradley Dorne," Josh said. "I don't know who he works for. We were following Aliyev..." Josh stopped short. His mind was having trouble catching up to everything that had happened in the last hour. It finally occurred to him something was way off.

"And?" the man in the tie asked.

"I don't know," Josh said, "I think I'm in shock, here."

"Jesus," the man said. "Let's get him in the vehicles. Put him in Charlie, and I'll interrogate as we go. There are two bodies in Alpha. Throw them in the fire."

Interrogate? Two dead bodies? Josh found himself hoping neither of the bodies was Dorne's.

Two men grabbed Josh under the arms, handcuffed his hands behind his back and hustled him to the last unscathed Suburban while three other men hauled two bodies out of the other Suburban and dragged them toward the fire. Josh sneaked a peek at the bodies as they shut the door on him. Both were in black tactical gear. Not Dorne, he thought.

Josh could see the man in the green tie through the front windshield. He surveyed the burning van and the dead bodies being tossed into the flames. One of the guys in black tactical gear handed him the broken 'terminators' Josh had been wearing. Tie man inspected the glasses then tossed them into the fire next to the two bodies. He made a circular motion in the air with his hand and turned to walk back to the Suburban. The rest of his crew began to go back to their respective vehicles. He opened the rear door across from Josh, looked at Josh, sighed and pulled out two more sets of handcuffs out of a holder on his belt.

"This is for your protection as well as mine," said tie man as he got in and leaned over to cuff Josh's ankles. When he finished cuffing his ankles, he took the cuffs on Josh's wrists and cuffed the bracelet to the chain between his ankles. Josh was now hogtied at an uncomfortable angle. The man left the door open and watched the rest of the men load up.

Joshua knew he needed to explain himself and the situation. "Sir," he began.

"Save it," tie man said with a wave of dismissal. "First, you will only answer questions I ask you, no more and no less. Understood?"

Josh nodded as well as he could with his head near his knees.

"Good," the man leaned back and surveyed the burning van. He motioned to the van and said, "As you can see; I mean business." He must have been talking about his men throwing the dead bodies into the fire. "Now," before the man could finish, a high coughing whine pierced the air. It sounded like a small faltering Cessna engine. The man and his men in black tactical gear looked up into the dark sky, and Josh cranked his neck to try and get a look through the front windshield. The sound grew louder and was coming closer from above.

"Major?" One of the men near the flaming van yelled at the leader. Tie man shot a look at the man standing near the blazing van, then went back to scanning the sky.

'Major Tie Man,' Josh thought. A deafening crash interrupted the thought. A gray object had emerged out of the dark sky and landed directly between the blazing van and Josh's Suburban. Pieces like giant Tinker-Toys shot out in every direction. A small propeller embedded itself in the bullet-resistant windshield of Josh's Suburban. Shards of fiberglass barely missed Josh's face and sunk into the seat backs behind him. Josh saw a piece of a small wing impale the man who had just addressed Major Tie. The rest of the men, including Major Tie, had dropped to the ground in time to save themselves from the flying shrapnel.

Major Tie slowly stood up, looked at the wreckage and muttered, "UAV. Now he's just fucking with us."

2200 HOURS, 24 OCTOBER 1998 – A61 AUTOBAHN, RHEINLAND-PFALZ

After the UAV crashed at the turnoff, Major Tie Man had ordered the men to throw the last body in the fire and pry out the propeller from his Suburban. His men in the black tactical gear had made quick work of both tasks, and they were immediately on their way. The convoy got back onto the B50 and crossed the border into Germany. At Prum they had taken the A1 back toward Cologne, and Major Tie Man told the driver to pick up the pace. Wind was coming through the foot long gash in the front windshield, chilling the Suburban. Major Tie Man hadn't yet spoken to Josh. He had his own mini-laptop and was pecking away. He seemed to have forgotten about his prisoner. At least they hadn't hooded him, Josh thought.

At one point, Major Tie Man produced the severed forearm and unwrapped it from another bundle of plastic. He laid it across his lap and pulled out a folding pen knife. He flipped the forearm palm up and proceeded to dig the knife into the fleshy portion just above the wrist. After about five minutes of digging, he pried out a small silver cylinder about the size of an aspirin. He examined it for a moment then gave it to the man in the front passenger seat, who put the cylinder in his shirt pocket. Major Tie Man then threw the mangled forearm into the back seat

When they took the E57 north out of Cologne, Josh knew they weren't heading back to Belgium. Or if they were, they were taking the extreme long way. This autobahn led into The Netherlands, unless they were heading toward Dusseldorf.

Josh had gone over the events of the evening at least a dozen times, getting his story straight. But what was there to get straight? Everything had happened as it happened, and none of it made any sense. Aliyev was the bad guy. They had followed the bad guy, and Dorne had gotten him. Then *these guys*, obviously American, show up and try to take out Dorne. They took Josh prisoner, talked about interrogation and then whisked him off to parts unknown. Were they CIA? They couldn't be CIA since they had a Major with them, or could they? Josh didn't know enough about the shadowy CIA world. They couldn't be military, because they wouldn't have disposed of their own like they did. They knew Josh was military, but hadn't bothered to take that into consideration. The loops of illogic based on what Josh had known in his six years in the military took him nowhere. Every time he risked asking a question, Major Tie Man would silence him with a dismissive wave.

He tried to think about something, anything, else. The problem was Josh didn't have much of a life outside the military. He didn't even have a girlfriend. He worked out, but only from habit. One thing was sure about this situation: if the military was his life, his life was over. Beebe and his superiors would find a way to nail him to the wall for this. He'd lose his clearance, for sure. He knew if he got a chance to explain, it wouldn't matter. Everyone would see it the same way--he should have ended the mission when Chief Smith called off the follow. They were going to nail him for failing to obey a lawful order, and when it was fully investigated, he'd be court marshaled for his involvement in the homicides today. He was screwed. Josh ended up just shaking his head and trying to look out the side window in an attempt to take his mind off his predicament.

Major Tie Man suddenly clapped his laptop shut, turned to Josh and said, "Where were we?"

Josh turned from the window and craned his neck to look at Major Tie Man.

"Let me get this straight," he began, "you're a 'Special Agent'," he sneered at the title as he said it.

"Yes," answered Josh.

"And you're a Staff Sergeant."

"Yes."

"How is it you found yourself in this situation tonight?"

Josh recounted the day beginning with the briefing back in Mons where he first saw Dorne. He said Dorne's name, but consciously left out the fact he was in Somalia in 1993. He described the follow, and most of the information Dorne had provided. Josh left out the personal story and the conversations with Dorne along the way.

"What did you talk about for seven hours?" asked Major Tie Man.

Josh told Major Tie that Dorne hadn't spoken much. He spent most of his time in the back of the van. It was true, for the most part, thought Josh. Josh went on to tell Major Tie that Dorne had kept him the dark as to the aim of the surveillance mission. He recounted how Smith had called off the follow, but Josh changed the actual story when Major Tie asked why he had not obeyed the order. Josh said Dorne had forced him to stay with him, saying he outranked Smith.

As Josh spoke, Major Tie Man closely examined Josh's badge and credentials, taking them out of the case and bending the plastic and biting the badge. He also closely examined the contents of Josh's wallet, scrutinizing his military identification card and his Texas driver's license.

"Why don't you have any credit cards?" Major Tie asked.

"I've never had one," Josh answered.

Major Tie Man looked directly into Josh's eyes for a moment, and then dropped his eyes back to the contents of the wallet. "Go on," he said.

Josh recounted the makeshift raid on the house, leaving out the part about the case. When asked why he destroyed the van, Josh replied he had no idea that turning the lever would cause the van's destruction. Major Tie Man asked Josh if he had any formal combat training.

"I'm a Ranger," said Josh.

"No shit?" Major Tie Man tossed the wallet on the floorboard and slapped the man in the passenger seat on the shoulder. "We have a no shit Ranger, here!" He laughed sarcastically. "Tell me this, *Ranger*, since when do you conduct a crappy makeshift raid with only two individuals and no support? Goddam Rangers."

Josh hung his head and looked at his bare feet. Apparently the frigid air coming through the gash in the windshield and the shot up Suburbans following behind them hadn't made an impression of support to Major Tie Man. The way Josh saw it, Major Tie Man and his crew had their asses kicked this evening. Josh also hadn't seen the metal case, meaning Dorne likely had gotten away with the plutonium in hand. Josh decided to act despondent instead of confronting Major Tie Man with these facts. Josh could feel a bit of the old anger rising, but the burning in his neck, feet, ankles, hands and wrists kept the ringing and blindness at bay. Plus, the shit river he was currently mouth-deep in did not provide for making waves.

Major Tie Man went on to quiz him on the information on his military identification card and driver's license. Age, Social Security Number- he asked that one 10 times, driver's license number- 10 times as well, home of record address and date of birth. Major Tie Man also asked Josh his office and phone numbers, chain of command, and names of friends back in Texas over and over, making sure he gave the same ones every time. He then told Josh to recount the entire evening again.

By the time Josh recounted the story again, they had crossed into The Netherlands. Josh hazarded a question as to their destination.

"I've made arrangements to hand you over to Interpol in The Hague," Major Tie said matter-of-factly. "Pick up the pace," he said to the driver. "I want to make it there by midnight."

Josh jerked against his restraints and craned his neck toward Major Tie.

"What?"

"You're an accessory in aiding a fugitive, 'Special Agent'," Major Tie said, placing that sticky sarcasm on Josh's title. "Plus I think you're not telling me everything. We're going to let the Europeans have their way with you, and we'll monitor your responses along with their thorough records checks. If Interpol is good for anything, it's thorough checks. When they're done with you, they'll hand you over to military justice. If you're who you say you are, you have nothing to worry about, *Ranger*." He chuckled again.

2358 HOURS, 24 OCTOBER 1998 – DUTCH INTERPOL HEADQUARTERS, THE HAGUE, NETHERLANDS

Five Interpol agents were waiting in the processing area when they arrived. Major Tie Man had taken the cuffs off his ankles and wiped the blood and grime from Josh's face before he took him in the building. As they got out of the vehicle, Josh noticed none of the INTERPOL agents took note of the damage to the Suburbans. They were all focused on him.

Josh knew European law and their treatment of prisoners. He knew they'd handle him with kid gloves, but they'd drown him in bureaucracy. The processing would take at least a week. Then there would be charges, which would take at least a month to nail down. Then there would be further processing. Then there might or might not be a trial depending on how the powers-that-be decided how they'd apply the agreements and treaties of the Status of Military Forces in Europe. Then the US military would get involved. Then there would be another few months of processing. It might be up to two years before punishment was handed down. Europeans were known for crushing criminals with the bureaucracy of their justice systems. He knew they wouldn't rough him up, though. They'd give him plenty to eat, and plenty of rest. They'd also make sure he had access to lawyers. Josh didn't care about any of that. He was lost. The outcome didn't matter to him one way or another. His life was over, and he had nothing at which to point his finger in accusation. He'd made all the right decisions this day, to include caving in the door of that Citroen. This had been one of the best days of his life, yet also unequivocally the worst. Josh took comfort in one thought: Beebe was going to have a coronary. This little episode was likely going to ensure the captain's career destruction, courtesy of Staff Sergeant Joshua D. Quinn. Josh smiled a little inside at that thought. He'd become a cautionary tale for all military personnel in Europe. They'd make commercials about him on the Armed Forces Network.

The Interpol officers moved him through initial processing rather quickly. They took his personal identifying information, his prints and his DNA. Through a window in the processing area, Josh could see Major Tie Man giving his statement to the Interpol officers. Judging by the casual look of their conversation, Major Tie Man had worked with these guys often. He was sitting with his legs crossed with his hands interlocked over one knee. Occasionally he'd put his head back and laugh at something humorous the Interpol agent had said. At one point, Major Tie Man's eyes met Josh's. He held Josh's eyes for only a moment, winked at him, and went back to joking with the agent taking his statement.

After his initial processing, four agents escorted Josh out of the headquarters building and across the parking lot to a smaller brick building surrounded by a chain link fence topped with razor wire. When they reached the gate to the building, one of the agents opened a telephone box next to the entrance, picked up the phone and pressed a button. A moment later he said a few words in Dutch, and the gate was buzzed open. When they reached the door leading into the building, the agent repeated the process. Once inside, the four agents handed Josh over to three men in blue police uniforms. The three men had identical utility belts with pepper spray, multiple sets of handcuffs, radios and a black baton. The three guards took Josh through a series of heavy doors and into yet another processing room. They instructed Josh to remove his clothing and shoes, and to change into a lime green jumpsuit and white velcro sneakers they had laid out for him.

Since Josh had been compliant and silent during the process, the guards did not bother to put him in restraints or handle him in a rough fashion. Josh was completely resigned to the point of catatonia. The adrenaline dump was starting to hit him hard. Too much had happened in too short of an amount of time. He knew he'd have a chance to chew on the situation, and maybe some food, once they had locked him in his cell. After he was done changing, the guards gave him a set of linens, some personal hygiene items in a brown paper sack, and two changes of socks and underwear folded into the linens. They escorted him through two barred gates and into a hall of jail cells. They opened the third cell and instructed Josh to enter. Once Josh walked into the twelve foot by twelve foot cell, they simply closed the cell door and left Josh alone with his thoughts.

He unfolded his linens and put them on the bed. He then tested the toilet and sink, and then dropped down and did push-ups until his arms and chest cramped. He rolled over on his back and soaked in the cold of the concrete floor.

Instead of going over the events of the day, Josh elected to start the process of figuring out how he wound up in this cell. It wasn't difficult to decide where to start. This ultimately began the day his mother decided not to come home from work, leaving him alone with his alcoholic and unhinged father for the rest of his sophomore year in high school.

FORT LEAVENWORTH DISCIPLINARY BARRACKS, KANSAS

"Your Ranger buddies talked," a voice said from behind.

He was cuffed in the chair again, in a sterile interrogation room with a single dim light over his head. He could smell the battlefield all around him. Dust, gunpowder, charred flesh, ozone, smoke, blood, accelerant, death. He could also still taste the battle-- a tinge of copper and iron on the sides and back of his tongue, almost like putting a penny in the mouth as a child.

"Everyone's going to know what you did," the voice said.

A woman's voice spoke up as if to punctuate; "I knew he'd turn out like this."

Joshua tried to crane his head around to see from where the familiar voice came, but he was no longer in handcuffs. Now he was in a straight jacket with the straps tied tightly around the back of the metal chair.

"That's why I left," the woman said.

"Mom?" Josh asked as he tried to turn again.

Now he could hear the battle. Automatic weapons, the whine of Little Birds, thudding explosions, boots pounding on hard dirt, the crackling of radios garbled by the battle, screams of pain, commands screeched in foreign languages and then silenced by deafening roars.

"Sergeant Quinn, those people you mutilated were innocent civilians who'd done nothing to you," said the voice over the noise of the battle.

"Are they still fighting?" Joshua asked.

"That isn't your concern," his mother said. "You've blown it. You've amounted to nothing. I told my Dad you were nothing like him. Turns out I was right." She broke out in a fit of laughter.

He screamed in rage as he struggled against the straight jacket, thrashing until the chair started to tip. The noise of the battle started to reach a crescendo when he heard a familiar voice.

"Ranger! Ranger! Get back in the fight!" It was First Sergeant Germaine. Thank God. "Lay down a suppressing fire while the vehicle exfil back to the airfield. Quinn! What are you doing? Get back in the fight!"

Josh opened his mouth to give a 'roger', but no words came. His mother was still laughing behind him and the other voice was threatening another sort of punishment. He shut his eyes hard and yelled, "Are they still fighting out there? Let me go!"

It's them, son. No mistake. They don't live another day.

"No," Joshua said. "Make them let me go. I can make a difference."

You have to do it on your own.

"You're not going anywhere," the voice behind him reminded. "We've got you now, you're exposed and you won't be causing any more problems."

"Let me go," Josh answered.

You have to do it on your own.

"How?" Joshua asked the ephemeral voice. He looked down at the straight jacket. It wasn't there anymore. Neither were the handcuffs and chains. He stood up from the chair and flexed his hands. The battle raged ever harder behind him. Slowly he turned and saw only enemy faces with rage in their eyes staring back. His mother wasn't there. The investigator wasn't there. Only the dark faces. Joshua's hands curled into fists and his face contorted into a primitive snarl. A single tear ran down his cheek.

It's not an easy choice. Kill them, young man. Stop thinking and do it. They started this war.

As he crouched to charge, the hiss of an RPG zipped in from above and detonated at his feet. He fell into the abyss.

1945 HOURS, 28 OCTOBER 1998 – INTERPOL CONFINEMENT FACILITY, THE HAGUE, NETHERLANDS

"Umph!" This time it seemed instead of falling out of bed, he'd leapt headlong across the room in his sleep. He reached behind his head and rubbed the lump already forming where he'd landed on the back of his skull. He looked up at the three guards standing outside his cell, watching the spectacle.

"You need help?" One of the guards asked in broken English.

Joshua nodded and waved them off. This time hadn't been much different from the last three times he'd slept. At least the guards were getting used to his nightmares. The first time, he awoke to two guards half attempting CPR.

"Sorry," Joshua said as the guards backed away from the door to go back to their duties. He shook his head clear and went to the sink to splash water on his face.

The last three days had been a mind numbing process of meetings with lawyers, law enforcement entities ranging from Dutch police and military, Luxembourg police, German police and military, Belgian police and military, and even a representative from the French police. A well-dressed US embassy representative had checked in on Josh just once, but only to see if he was healthy. The embassy rep wasn't interested in Josh's story, only that Josh was being treated properly. He had yet to speak to a US military JAG officer, which he found disconcerting but typical.

Josh had told the same story at least a dozen times the first two days. Every lawyer and police officer seemed to only be concerned with the fact

65

they had continued on the follow after hearing there had been a multiple homicide in Brussels. When Josh mentioned the plutonium, every representative seemed to cringe and shy away from follow-up questions. The military reps were mainly concerned with the weapons found on Josh and how he got them. Each military rep rattled off the same list of military firearm bans, of which there were hundreds Josh had violated. The military reps had the same reaction to the plutonium, but seemed to be more disbelieving that their civilian counterparts. The military reps also completely dismissed the existence of the Little Bird and the UAV. Even when Josh asked the Luxembourg police what kinds of round casings they had found at the Akescht farmhouse, the representative dodged the question.

By the third day, the police and military reps seemed to have all they wanted from him, and Josh was only talking to prosecutors and prospective defense counselors. At this point, the lawyers focused only on the chain of events from Mons, Belgium to Maastricht, The Netherlands. They were obviously building a case on the double homicide and trying to figure out the level of negligence on Josh's part. Despite his insistence that they hear and heed the rest of the story from Maastricht to Akescht, both prosecuting and defense lawyers refused to acknowledge the events. They cited numerous European Union and Interpol codes, but Josh knew enough about law to understand the events occurring between Maastricht and Akescht had somehow been sealed. For all intents and purposes, they never happened nor did they matter. Now he wasn't being held for aiding in the escape of Bradley Dorne, because the events surrounding Bradley Dorne didn't exist in the eyes of the courts. As far as the courts were concerned, Josh had been driving an empty van the whole day on 24 October 1998. Anything involving missing plutonium, armed Little Birds buzzing across the European countryside, severed arms and shadowy non-state actors who speak multiple languages were just too troubling for the counselors and their respective governments.

When they took him back to his cell at the end of the day, Josh was just as confused as he was 96 hours ago when Major Tie Man and his crew had shown up right before the van went up in flames. Perhaps confused was not the right word, Josh realized. He knew the reasons they changed the focus of their allegations, but he was not any closer to figuring out who the players had been and why they had acted as they had. Major Tie was American for sure--he had that military or ex-military swagger, and he had that Beebe-esque disdain for Rangers. Dorne, on the other hand, could be Canadian. Josh heard stories about some Canadian Special Forces in Somalia supporting the SEALs, but he seemed more American than Canadian. Why were Dorne and Major Tie Man not on the same team?

He pondered the question as he knocked out pushups. He was on his sixth set of 50 when a guard dragged his baton across the bars of Josh's cell.

"You have another appointment," one of them said in a heavy Dutch accent.

Josh got up and went to the sink to grab his towel. "Another one? Who is it this time?" Josh asked as he wiped the sweat from his face and neck.

"Unexpected meeting with US defense counsel," the guard said.

"Finally." Josh threw the towel in the sink and approached the cell door.

The guards escorted Josh to the same antiseptic smelling room where he'd already met with dozens of reps, expect this time the defense counsel was not waiting for him. They told Josh to have a seat and wait as they closed the door behind him. Josh walked to the far end of a long single table and sat down where the counsel usually sat, with their backs to the two-way mirrored glass. He got comfortable in the chair and turned around to look up at the cameras in each corner behind him. As usual the green lights at the corners of the cameras were on, recording. He turned around and spun the chair to the side so he could put his feet up on the table. He rested his hands behind his head and closed his eyes.

About ten minutes later, he heard the lock on the door turning. Josh pivoted his legs off the table and turned his chair back square with the table. A Hispanic Lieutenant Colonel in a Dress Green uniform entered and walked to the chair opposite of Josh without acknowledging him. His name tape read 'Flores', and his fruit salad award ribbon rack was almost bare. The door closed and locked as Lieutenant Colonel Flores set his briefcase on the table and opened it. He shuffled some papers inside the briefcase, took out a thick file folder, closed the briefcase and sat down. He opened the file folder and perused some of the items including what looked to be overhead imagery of the European countryside, possibly taken from a low flying airplane. Lieutenant Colonel Flores still hadn't acknowledged Josh as he perused the contents of the file folder. He picked up one photograph of the severed arm, held it up to the light and grunted in disapproval. "Very sloppy," he said with a thick Mexican accent. He still would not look directly at Josh.

Josh joined his hands, leaned forward and put his forearms on the table. "Yes sir, this whole situation is sloppy."

"Mm-hm," Lieutenant Colonel Flores mumbled as he continued to study the contents of the file folder. "What questions do you have of me, soldier?" Flores's accent was so thick his R's rolled.

"I guess my first question is; exactly how much trouble am I in, here?"

Flores continued to study images from the case file. "What makes you think you're in any kind of trouble, cabrone?"

Josh was taken aback. He grew up in Texas, and he knew what 'cabrone' meant. That's unprofessional, he thought, what kind of JAG officer have they given him? "Sir?"

"Mm-hm?" Flores looked up at Josh and met his eyes for the first time.

Josh leaned in, cocked his head to the side and studied Flores's face. Flores winked at Josh. "Wait a minute!" Josh exclaimed in a loud whisper. He turned around and looked at the camera over his left shoulder. No green light. He pivoted and checked the one over his right shoulder. No green light. He glanced at the two-way glass, but quickly turned around and leaned his elbows on the table with his head down. "How in the hell did you get in here?"

The Lieutenant Colonel chuckled in reply.

Josh looked up from the table and leaned further over the surface toward the Lieutenant Colonel. He asked in a whisper; "Who *are* you?"

Bradley Dorne replied with a thick Mexican accent, "At the moment I'm Lieutenant Colonel Rodrigo Flores, your US Army JAG attorney."

2050 HOURS, 28 OCTOBER 1998 – INTERPOL CONFINEMENT FACILITY, THE HAGUE, NETHERLANDS

Josh sat in stunned silence as Dorne said something about not worrying about cameras or listening devices in the room, and to just speak normally as he would any other lawyer.

"Hey! Hey! You Listening to me, kid?" There was no longer any hint of a Mexican accent.

Josh shook his head as if to clear it and looked up. "What?"

"Pull yourself together," Dorne said. "Did your feet every thaw?" He looked under the table at Josh's shoes.

"Yeah. Sorry, it's just you're the last person I expected to see in here," Josh said, still shaking his head.

"And why is *that*?"

Josh looked at Dorne, puzzled. "Let me list the reasons."

Dorne sighed, obviously exasperated; "Do you remember one of the last things I told you? I said, 'I'll find you and make all this right,' and you said, 'yeah'. You don't remember that?"

"That was before everything went to shit."

"What difference does that make?" Dorne asked. "I said I'd do something and here I am. Now making this right will depend a great deal on how this conversation goes."

Josh was still only half listening to Dorne. He was examining Dorne's polish, or disguise. The skin darkening agent Dorne had used was perfectly even with no hint of make-up dust and buildup. He had tinted his hair with gray streaks, added worry lines in his forehead and made the crow's feet at the outer corners of his eyes a bit more pronounced. He'd changed his eye color to dark brown, but Josh couldn't see the outline of contacts. He looked at Dorne's hands and saw the darkening agent was perfectly blended there, as well. Amazing.

"Hey! Hey!" Dorne snapped his fingers in the air in front of Josh's face. "Up here! Damn, this already isn't going well."

"Sorry. Sorry. I'm listening."

"Alright," Dorne cocked his head to the side, then back forward as if to reset the conversation. "I've been doing this for a long time, and you're a kid with about three days of combat experience. So I imagine you have a lot of questions. We'll get to those in time. This conversation is going to be about you. I'm going to ask you a lot of questions, and you'll answer them. I'm going to also do a lot of talking, so listen closely and you might find some answers." Dorne stopped to take a look at his watch, then continued; "We only have a few hours here. So let's see if I can hold true to my word of making this right. You ready?"

"I am."

Dorne leaned over his open briefcase and pulled out a legal pad and a Mont Blanc pen. He wrote a few notes at the top in short hand. He gathered the open case file and placed it back in a pocket inside the briefcase. He then pulled out another case file, laid it on the table, opened the file and looked back up at Josh. He cleared his throat and began; "I've been very busy over the last 96 hours or so. I spent a good deal of that time digging into your past," he motioned to the open file in front of him, "as you can see. I now literally know more about you than your own mother." He stopped abruptly and studied Josh's reaction to the comment. Josh remained focused on Dorne and showed no signs of negative emotion.

"Mm-hm," Dorne murmured as he flipped back the first page on the left hand side of the file. "Looks to me like you're some kind of golden-boy superstar. In high school you lettered in track, football and wrestling. You also graduated in the top five percent of your class. You accomplished all this with an alcoholic father who had a record of assault and battery, and a mother who left home to shack up with a methamphetamine dealer and then ended up bouncing in and out of prison until she died of an overdose..." he flipped another page, "during Spring Break of your senior year." Dorne looked up at Josh again to gauge his reaction. Josh just nodded slightly and remained solemnly focused on Dorne.

"You received a football scholarship to Southwest Texas State University where you studied law. You'd told me that on our adventure. What you didn't mention is that the scholarship was partial and you violated NCAA rules when you took two part time jobs waiting tables at a steakhouse in New Braunfels, and stocking shelves at a grocery store in San Marcos. In the summers you worked full time at a water park, which wasn't against the rules, but a *lifeguard*, Joshua?" Dorne looked up and gave Josh a disapproving nod.

Josh shrugged his shoulders and said, "Scenery."

Dorne continued, "You played football all four years and started two of those years. You set the bench press and 40 yard dash record for the strong safety position, which still stands at Southwest Texas State. Bravo on that. What else?" Dorne flipped another page. " You weren't a member of a social fraternity, but you were member of Phi Sigma Tau, the international philosophy honor society. You graduated Cum Laude with a degree in political science. You paid your rent on time in every shithole you lived in while in college. I saw pictures of the Shady Acres apartment complex. I'm surprised you weren't stabbed to death while residing there."

Josh nodded.

"Mm-hm," Dorne continued. "But there is the little matter about the fight that got you in so much trouble. It seems, according to the court documents and police report, that it wasn't a fight in a parking lot at all. There were three Hispanic men involved, though. You went to their house and you raised hell. None of them were minors, and you actually killed one." Dorne flipped yet another page, and Josh lowered his eyes and leaned back in his chair. "The court documents say it was self-defense, but damn! These police report crime scene photos are pretty gruesome. You want to tell me the truth about that night?"

Without looking up, Josh began; "Like you said; my dad was an alcoholic. He was never around much for me or my sister Vic, but he went to work at the fiberglass plant most nights and paid the bills. He was a violent guy, but not usually with me and never with Vic. You know about my mother. Before she died, none of us had seen or heard from her in months. Even though she and Vic weren't close, when she died, Vic lost it. It was her sophomore year and my senior year, like you said. Basically, Vic fell in with the wrong crowd. I decided to go off to college instead of staying home, thinking everything would work itself out. I thought it was just a phase for Vic. Every time I went home to visit, Vic was around less and less often. I heard about what she was doing less and less. During my junior year at Southwest Texas State, I got word that she'd been busted with four grams of meth. I went home to try and talk it over with my dad, but he was in no shape to reason through anything. So I made an offer to Vic-- come live with me in San Marcos to get away from the influences back home.

"She took me up on my offer and I rented out a one bedroom efficiency at Shady Acres. She got a job at the Wal-Mart in San Marcos, stayed out of trouble and was even thinking about trying to go to college. The last half of my senior year, everything went to hell with her. She fell in love with a guy from her work and started hanging out with his crew. I noticed her coming in later and later, sometimes staying away from the apartment for days. When she would come home, it would be to crash for a few days. I knew she wasn't working anymore. When I confronted her and reminded her of our mother, she's blow up and disappear with her boyfriend for days. I guess I should have tried harder to keep her out of trouble..." Josh stopped. He cleared his throat, folded his hands and put them on the table. He still hadn't looked up.

"Mm-hm," Dorne could see Josh's knuckles turning white through his folded hands. "Go on."

Josh cleared his throat again and continued, "I hadn't seen her in three weeks. I had no idea where she was. I was assuming she was with her boyfriend on a bender somewhere. I justified not looking for her by saying to myself she was an adult and it was her life and her choice. That night, I was at a party celebrating our graduation and my law school acceptance. During the party, one of my buddies took me aside and said he'd seen Vic the day before our graduation. He said he'd seen her rummaging through a dumpster behind the Safeway on Broad street. He told me she looked like she'd lost 30 pounds, that her clothes were in tatters, and that she'd shaved her head. Vic had always loved her hair. She had this thick and wavy auburn hair that went down to her waist. She'd always taken care of her hair. She'd spend hours styling it, curling it, straightening it. Right there in the bar, I started to have one of my 'attacks'. I remember leaving the bar, but I don't remember a thing after that until I arrived at her boyfriend's house in the Heights. I didn't go over there to hurt anyone. I went to find out where Vic was.

"When her boyfriend Rico opened the door, I grabbed him by the shirt and dragged him into the front yard. I kept yelling, 'Where's Victoria? Where's Victoria?' I threw him down on the ground and kept yelling, 'Where's Victoria? Where's Victoria?' It must have been quite a sight for Rico, because he kept crawling like a crab away from me. I remember as I was yelling down at Rico, I heard the screen door behind me open and slam shut. A second later, a baseball bat caught me across the lower back and dropped me. I remember them kicking me while I was on the ground. I covered up and took the kicks until I recovered from the kidney shot. I grabbed a leg and took one of them down. The other two kept kicking, but I put the guy in a choke and rolled so he was absorbing most of the kicks. When I felt him go limp, I let go and got to my feet. Rico backed off a little and said something in Spanish to his buddy. His buddy took a swing at me with the bat and Rico sprinted back to the house. I went at the guy with the bat and absorbed a swing with my forearms.

"Judging by the sound of the crack, I knew the hit had probably broken my arm, but I couldn't feel a thing. As the guy tried to raise the bat for another swing, I tackled him and drove him head first into the sidewalk. I felt him go limp, so I stood back up. I picked up the bat and turned toward the house. Out walked Rico with a pistol pointed directly at my chest.

Josh leaned back in his chair and spread his arms, "Look at me, Dorne. I'm not a small guy. Rico with his scrawny, drugged out ass knew the only way he could beat me was with a gun. I'm sure he felt threatened, and he came out of that house looking to kill me. I could see it in his eyes. I didn't hesitate. I threw the bat end over end at him. He raised his arms and turned to the side. The bat hit him in the shoulder, tumbled and hit him in the side of the head. As he went to his knees, he pulled the trigger. The report of the shot didn't even register with me because I was already bull rushing him. His knees had just hit the ground when I wrapped him up and drove him through the screen door and into the house. He was unconscious when he hit the ground. I hauled him up and shook him until , he started to regain consciousness. With his eyes half open, he started mumbling, 'sorry, sorry, sorry. Don't kill me. Sorry.' I threw him back to the ground and stood over him yelling, 'Where's Victoria? Where's Victoria?'

"He motioned toward a hallway leading to bedrooms. He was still slurring; 'Sorry. Don't kill me. Sorry.' Before I went down the hallway, I went out on the porch, picked up the pistol and tucked it into the back of my jeans. I went back in the house and raged passed Rico and down the hall screaming 'Victoria! Vicky!' Turning over tables, knocking over chairs, and slamming doors open. When I reached the third bedroom, I kicked the door open. There was Vic."

Josh unfolded his hands and laid his palms flat on the table. He looked up and to the left. Dorne could see Josh's eyes were growing misty, but he didn't let up; "Go on."

Josh lowered his head again and cleared his throat twice. "There was Vic. Completely naked and stretched out on the bed spread eagle. She was so skinny the most dominating features on her body were her protruding hip bones. Frozen where I stood, I could see her chest rising and falling so I knew she was alive. Her arms were tied at the wrists to the headboard, and her legs tied at the ankles to the foot board, stretching her pasty, sick skin across her ribs. There were no sheets or covers on the bed, and the mattress was filthy. The room reeked of sex. I gagged and went down to a knee, but I quickly gathered myself and staggered to the bed. I tried to rouse her by gently stroking her head and saying her name. She was so out of it, but after a moment she barely opened her eyes and looked at me. All she said was, 'No more. Please. No more. Please stop.' I looked back up at my hand stroking her bald head and remembered her beautiful hair she'd once had.

"I remember untying her. I remember taking off my shirt and covering her as best I could. I remember walking into the kitchen and dialing 911 and not saying anything. I remember putting the phone down on the kitchen counter, reaching around my waist and gripping the pistol. I very deliberately walked into the living room where Rico was sitting, nursing his shoulder. I very calmly stood over him and told him to open his mouth. The next thing I remember was being stood up, cuffed and walked to the police cruiser parked in the front yard, just feet from the porch.

"I knew enough about Miranda not to say a damn thing when I was arrested. During trial, the prosecution said I had put the gun in Rico's mouth and pulled the trigger, but defense said ballistics to support this claim were weak. My defense lawyer was brilliant. He made the case about crime of passion, and submitted Vic's medical records. Listening to him list her internal injuries from multiple rapes, her malnourishment to the point of starvation and the laundry list of narcotics in her system almost sent me into a rage right there in the courtroom.

"He managed to make the 911 call inadmissible. Based on my very censored and coached testimony, the jury determined the shooting was self defense. They stuck me with assault on one of the Rico's buddies, citing the severity of his paralysis. That's when the judge gave me the military option. Despite my defense attorney's wishes to fight on, I elected to join the military. At the time, the only branch that would take me was the Army."

Josh sat up and raised his eyes to meet Dorne's. There was no longer mist in Josh's eyes. Dorne saw Josh had replaced grief with anger and rage. "There. That's it. Now you know more than the state of Texas. What does this have to do with anything that's happened in the last few days? Have I earned answers yet?"

Dorne broke Joshua's stare to casually check his watch. He glanced up at Josh, then back into the file. "Not yet," he said.

2200 HOURS, 28 OCTOBER 1998 – INTERPOL CONFINEMENT FACILITY, THE HAGUE, NETHERLANDS

Josh shook his head and stared over Dorne's shoulder. Dorne noticed Josh had pulled his lower lip between his teeth and was gnashing on it.

"Hey!" Dorne snapped. Josh looked back at him. "Calm down. Relax. This is not a trial or an Article 15 hearing. I have a lot of ground to cover. I still have questions, and you owe me answers. Believe it or not, that's how this goes."

Josh nodded his head and folded his arms across his chest. Dorne took a moment to study Josh again. The anger and rage had come and gone, and he was back in compliance mode. Dorne narrowed his eyes, then turned back to the file. "Now," he said, continuing on as if Josh had not just told a gut-wrenching life changing event, "Does it bother you at all that you gave a false report to the police and perjured yourself in court?"

"No," Josh answered.

"Why not?" Dorne readied his pen at the legal pad next to the file.

"I was justified in almost every objective sense, and I didn't deserve punishment."

"You killed a man..."

"That deserved to die," Josh interrupted.

Dorne finished his thought without acknowledging Josh's interjection; "...who did not have the opportunity to be judged by way of trial."

"He deserved to die, trial or no." Josh leaned back and raised his chin as if challenging Dorne.

"Explain."

Josh unfolded his arms and leaned forward toward Dorne, looking him in the eye; "I have an acute sense of justice as well as injustice. So do you. We can smell our own."

For the first time, Dorne leaned back away from the table. He stared at Josh, amazed. He narrowed his eyes again and glanced down at the file, then his notes. Obviously not finding what he wanted, he looked back up at Josh and studied him again for a moment. Josh didn't shrink from the scrutiny. Dorne regained his composure and leaned forward again. "Can you read shorthand?"

"No," Josh answered.

"'An acute sense of justice and injustice'. Why did you choose those words?"

"Because it's the truth," Josh said.

"Yes, but why those words?"

Josh shrugged. "I don't know. Those words pretty much sum it all up. Is there another way to say it?"

"I guess not," Dorne answered, "it's just...no. We'll get to that later." Dorne scribbled a few more notes and without looking up said; "Let's say your career wasn't almost over right now. Would you stay in the military?"

"Yes. Hell, I'll probably stay in and try to repair the damage if they'll let me."

"You see," Dorne leaned back and put his hands behind his head, sighed and said, "that's what I'm having trouble figuring out," he motioned to the file on the table with his elbow, "Your psych profile there says you're ambitious and unlikely as well as unwilling to accept unsolicited or solicited assistance. In other words, you're not a slacker who wants a free ride. There also isn't anything in your record to indicate you are overly patriotic. In my experience, there are three types of people in the military: slackers who need Uncle Sugar to give them a ride until retirement, patriotic true-believers, and finally the people who have nowhere else to go. The people who have nowhere else to go will usually stay in, but you're not one of those. You could easily make it on the civilian side; you know it and I know it. I trust the psyche profile's assessment that you're not a slacker. So what's with the patriotic stuff? Tell me about that."

"My granddad," Josh said. "My mom's dad. When Vic and I were very young, we'd stay with him and work on his farm in the summers. It wasn't really much of a farm, just 250 acres about 15 miles outside of Brownwood, Texas. He was from the old school. He'd make us work all day in the blistering heat doing every sort of manual labor; bailing hay, cutting grass, digging post holes, everything. In the evenings, he'd make us read books on American history and the Constitution then he'd sit down and quiz us on what we had learned. If we did well on the quizzes, he'd tell me some of his war stories. When he turned 16 in 1944, he lied about his age and enlisted in the Marine Corps. After Boot Camp, they sent him to the Pacific theater for the duration of the War. When he got back to the States, he decided to make a career out of the Marine Corps. He was stationed in San Diego and that's where he met my grandmother. They had a four years together before Korea kicked off. Just before he had to leave to go fight that war, my mother was born. He got to be there for the birth, but a week later he was gone. He stayed and fought in Korea all three years. He was directly commissioned while in Korea and came back a Captain.

"When he returned from Korea, he was posted at the Pentagon. Then in 1963 he was sent to Vietnam as a military adviser to the ARVN. By 1970, he had pulled five tours in Vietnam, and was on his sixth. On 21 March 1970, my birthday, a mortar round hit his Command Post at Fire Base Danger in the Din Tuong Province. It blew his left leg clean off at the hip. He was medically separated as a Major when he finished his recovery in 1972. He regretted what he saw as an early end to his career, but he always said he was lucky to be alive. Vic never wanted to see them, but when I asked he'd always show me the scars running up and down the left side of his torso. He never once complained about his missing leg, and despite his handicap he'd work circles around me and Vic every summer. The funny thing was when he'd tell the story of how he lost his leg, he'd always go off on a tangent about working for Lieutenant Colonel Hackworth when he was attached to the 4/39 Infantry Recondo Company."

"No shit?" Dorne interjected, "Colonel Hackworth's outfit?"

"Yeah. You know about it?" Josh asked.

"I do. Sorry for the interruption. Go ahead." Dorne motioned for him to continue.

"I learned more from my granddad during the summers than I learned in the entirety of my formal public education. He taught me how to work and the value of a solid work ethic. He taught me how to shoot and handle weapons. He taught me the importance of the US Constitution and Bill of Rights. He taught me how blessed I am to be born in the US, and that I should thank God every day for that blessing. Most importantly, he taught me I have a duty and a responsibility to serve the country. It's true I studied law, but my aim was to be in the FBI."

"Aw, pft," Dorne snorted, "You made the right bargain going military, Joshua. But why did you go Army? Why not the Marines? And what about your grandmother? Does she play a part in this story?"

"When I'd tell my granddad I wanted to be a Marine like him, he'd always wink and say the same thing: 'Don't sell yourself short, J.D.'"

Dorne looked up from his notes. "'J.D.'?"

"My middle name starts with a 'D'," said Josh. "Only Vic and my granddad called me J.D."

Dorne nodded.

"Yeah, so he told me not to sell myself short. I always took that to mean he thought I had more to offer than military service, so that's why I decided to pursue the FBI. When that career choice came to a crashing halt, I didn't have a chance to go back and ask him what he meant by 'selling myself short'. He died of a heart attack just after my mother overdosed. Which brings me to my grandmother. She died of ovarian cancer when I was three."

Josh pointed at the file next to Dorne's notepad and said, "What that file might not tell you is that I'm a bastard. At 19, my mother let a sailor on shore leave in Virginia knock her up while my granddad was in Vietnam. He actually named me. Things were different back then. Getting knocked up was a big deal and most times, abortion was out of the question. My grandparents kept it quiet and helped raise me. After my grandmother died, my granddad moved us back to Brownwood where my mother met that piece of shit who called himself my father. He legally adopted me and changed my last name to Quinn. Then they had my sister, which was the only decent thing to come out of their union. We would have lived with my granddad, but my step father wouldn't let us go. He stood to lose about a thousand dollars a year if he gave us up as dependents, and he wasn't about to do that. I suppose it is too late to make a long story short, but I do what I do and I think what I think because I want to make my granddad proud."

Dorne nodded his head and asked, "What was his name?"

"Major Joshua Dante Sabol, III, United States Marine Corps, Retired."

2315 HOURS, 28 OCTOBER 1998 – INTERPOL CONFINEMENT FACILITY, THE HAGUE, NETHERLANDS

Dorne sat for a moment in silence, recognizing the influence of Joshua's grandfather on his life. He knew this last section of the evaluation would be tricky. He'd prepared for years, but he'd never actually done it. Just before he began, Dorne realized this would likely be his first and last chance, and he only had about two more hours. This kid could be the one, he thought, and I have to get it right. Dorne didn't want to press him again, but he had to do it. He didn't look up from his notes as he began, "Joshua, do you think your grandfather's absence had anything to do with how all of this turned out? Your mother getting pregnant, for instance."

"Absolutely," Josh said immediately, then he thought for only a moment and qualified his answer; "but everyone makes their own choices in the end, and they're responsible for the consequences of their choices. So I can't blame my granddad, even though the older I got he'd often say he blamed himself for how things had turned out for me and Vic and our mother. He'd say the same thing you asked--that if he would have been around more, maybe he could have positively influenced my mother's decisions, including the choice to marry my 'dad'."

"Mm-hm," Dorne said as he wrote in the pad, "and how does that knowledge guide your life now?"

Josh gave a snorted chuckle and said, "You asked if I was gay a couple of days ago. Man, I like women just as much as the next guy, but I'll be honest and say it isn't easy for me to keep relationships going. Once I do get to that relationship point, I end up pulling away. I know myself well enough to understand I want to make my granddad proud, but I don't want to make his mistakes. The only mistakes he ever made were the ones he couldn't control because he didn't know any better. I know better. I see, even at a subconscious level, that duty and relationships do not mix. All you have to do is look at the divorce rate for military families. Are you married?"

"No," Dorne blurted.

"See? You get it," Josh said.

Dorne recovered from his immediate response and kept going; "What about close friendships?"

"I see them in the same light as romantic relationships," Josh said. "I have no problem establishing friendships, but I end up pulling away. I see it in myself, and I suppose it is a problem, but I believe I'm saving myself, and these potential best friends and girlfriends, a lot of pain. At least that's how I justify it to myself."

So far, so good, Dorne thought. Josh hadn't taken the bait on the emotionally charged questions, and all his answers were spot on. Spooky spot on, Dorne noted. He wrote a few more notes then said, "Alright. I have a few more questions. These will require short answers. You've been open and honest with me thus far, and I appreciate it. So I need not tell you to answer honestly. Ready?"

Josh nodded.

"When was the last time you were late to a formation or a military movement?"

"The morning of the surveillance. The day I met you," Josh answered.

"How many times in your career have you been late to a formation or a military movement?"

"Three, including the last time."

"Over the last five years, how many times have you gone to the hospital?"

"Twice. Both times were related to the injuries I sustained in Mogadishu," Josh said.

Dorne jotted a note as he asked, "Do you take any prescription medication?"

"Not currently."

"Do you use any illegal narcotics of any sort?"

"No."

"Have you ever used any illegal narcotics of any sort?"

"Yes."

"When?"

"My freshman of college, then again between my sophomore and junior year."

"What kind?"

"I smoked marijuana a few times my freshman year. Then I used steroids between my sophomore and junior year."

Dorne scribbled a few notes, then looked up and asked, "Why did you use the steroids?"

"To make the team. To keep my scholarship."

Dorne scribbled more notes. He had to throw something in to try to trip this kid up. "When was the last time you had sex?"

Josh exhaled through pursed lips and looked up and to the left. "With another person? Whew. Let's see. I can't say for sure...let's see...about ten months ago? It was the last time I went back to Brownwood. Old high school flame who'd recently divorced."

"Mm-hm." It's time to drop the bombs, Dorne thought. Again, he didn't look up as he asked; "When was the last time you saw Victoria?"

Josh didn't hesitate, "At my trial before I joined the Army when she was a witness."

"How often do you talk to her?"

"Never."

"Do you know where she is?"

"No."

"Would you like to see her again?"

"Not really," Josh shrugged and folded his arms across his chest.

Dorne pulled out a letter sized manila envelope out of the briefcase and tossed it toward Josh. It slid directly in front of Josh's crossed arms. Josh looked down at it. Written in black marker were the words 'Victoria Anne Quinn'.

"You sure?" Dorne asked.

Josh slowly unfolded his arms, put one hand on the envelope and slid it back in front of Dorne. "Yes."

Dorne couldn't help himself, "Right answer." He smirked a bit. This was going to work out.

"Last question of the series, Joshua," Dorne said. He pushed his notes aside. "What is your prized possession? What's inside that cold little row house in Biamont you can't live without?"

Josh refolded his arms and looked up at the ceiling, squinting his eyes. He thought for about fifteen seconds, then answered, "My punching bag."

Dorne dropped his pen and began laughing, and Josh joined in.

"Seriously?" Dorne said through his laughter.

"I guess so," Josh said.

Dorne realized he had needed that laugh, but he wasn't laughing at the absurdity of the prized possession. He was laughing at how absurdly perfect Joshua D. Quinn's story and answers had been. The rest of the interview should be a slam-dunk. Dorne kept his notes to the side. They didn't matter anymore, anyway. He looked up at Josh and said, "Alright Joshua, you've been a good sport so far. If I were in your place, I don't know if I would have been able to keep it together with all the questions swirling around up there," he pointed at Josh's head and made a waving motion with the pen in his hand. "Remember back in the day when you said Delta thought you were damaged goods due to the results of the psychological evaluation?"

"Yes," Josh answered.

"Well, they were half right," Dorne said. He opened the file back up and flipped a few pages. "I have the evaluation right here, and I put it through my own analysis. Turns out, they were right in that you don't fit the profile to be a Delta operator. But," he held up on finger, "you are not damaged goods, kid. The purpose of the interview I just gave was to make a final determination on your overall mental state. Mental health is a tricky science, and there are so many factors involved in making any sort of diagnosis. My organization uses an amalgamation of both the International Statistical Classification of Diseases, or the ICD-10, and the Diagnostic and Statistical Manual of Mental Disorders, or DSM-IV-TR. From these two sources, we have added our own environmental factors that affect certain individuals in certain career fields. The result is a hybrid mental state that we do not classify as a disorder. Are you following me?"

"I think so," Josh said.

"Good," Dorne continued, "Let me put it this way: There are certain highly functional individuals with autism who can fully function in society, albeit with certain difficulties. Some of these individuals are chess masters, scientists, mathematicians or nuclear physicists. Yet according to the ICD-10 and the DSM-IV-TR, they are classified as having 'disorders'. Obviously, you are not autistic. Joshua, you have a condition we label 'Egosyntonic Axis IV Sociopathy', or 'EA IV S'."

Josh tilted his head as if he didn't understand. "A sociopath? Like Dahmer or Bundy?"

"No," Dorne answered, "not like them. Those men were Psychopaths with Sociopathic tendencies and behaviors. You're missing the point. You've been diagnosed with something *positive*. It's like being diagnosed with a muscle structure that make you stronger and faster than an average athlete, or a frontal lobe of your brain that is shaped in such a way that makes you able to process information faster than an average scholar. Most of the truly great professional boxers like Joe Frasier, for instance, have a chemical imbalance in their brains making their knockout threshold higher than an average man's. Get it?"

Josh nodded, but seemed a bit shaken.

"Look," Dorne said, "You said the magic words early in the interview. You said, 'I have an acute sense of justice as well as injustice'. I had to make sure you weren't quoting from my shorthand notes. Our diagnosis is based on an individual first having, and I quote," Dorne pulled his notes in up and read; "...'an acute sense of justice and injustice directly applied to the diagnosed disorders within Trait Cluster Zulu, resulting in an egosyntonic condition...'" Dorne pushed his notes aside and turned back to Josh. "Simply put, you have a certain set of conditions some would classify as a disorder, but when viewed through the lens of an acute sense of justice and injustice, those conditions become assets for us. Without that lens, the individual is simply a sociopath, or possibly a psychopath."

Josh nodded his head slightly and stared almost blankly at Dorne's chest. Finally he asked, "What is Trait Cluster Zulu, and what the hell does 'egosyntonic' mean?"

He's on the hook, Dorne thought. "Good question," he said. "There are six very specific behavioral traits that make up Trait Cluster Zulu. Some of these traits tie into one another, but remember; each trait must be analyzed through the lens of that 'acute sense of justice and injustice' about which we've spoken." Dorne reached for the notes and read from them. "The first is a persistent attitude of disregard for rules and norms. The second is an incapacity to maintain enduring relationships, but no difficulty in establishing them. The third is a very low tolerance to frustration and a low threshold for discharging aggression, including violence. The fourth is and incapacity to experience guilt or remorse. The fifth is characterized by a penchant for deception as indicated by lying or using aliases. The sixth is a reckless disregard for safety of self." Dorne put the notes down and said, "Does that sound like someone you know?"

"Not me," Josh said.

Dorne rolled his eyes. "Sure it is. I've only looked through your file and spoken with you for a few hours total, and I can see this is you all over."

Josh shook his head and asked, "How is that? What you just outlined sounds like you're describing a piece of crap. I know I've had my share of problems, but I'm not a *total* piece of crap. Despite what Captain Beebe might tell you."

"Exactly!" exclaimed Dorne, "Exactly! That polished piece of West Point garbage would tell me you're a trouble maker! A loose cannon. A soldier with no regard for the rules. What was the first rule I saw you break? You took that pistol from me when I offered it. You knew it was against regulations and that Beebe had in effect disarmed you for no reason relating to your ability to responsibly handle a weapon. You knew taking it was the right thing to do, but you also knew you were breaking the rules. An incapacity to maintain relationships. You told me yourself not ten minutes ago you had trouble with that. A low tolerance to frustration? Come on, Josh. You have a long record of aggression and violence, but remember; in every case, you were justified. You feel no guilt or remorse for the actions you have taken that most of society would view as extreme, such as breaking that young man's spine, or blowing a hole in Rico's head. But for you, those actions are righteously justified, therefore you feel no remorse or guilt. A penchant for lying? You lied at your trial, you've lied to me, you've lied to these people," Dorne motioned at the two way glass behind Josh, then at the cameras, "and they believe you. I'm guessing you lied to the guy who picked you up in Luxembourg and brought you here, as well. Finally, a reckless disregard for safety of self. I think this," Dorne pulled a piece of paper out of the file and set it in front of Josh, "speaks for itself."

Josh looked down at the paper. It was his DD-214 military record listing his decorations. He looked back up at Dorne, arms still crossed. Dorne reached and pulled the paper back in front of himself and read; "Silver Star with 'Valor' device, two Bronze Stars both with 'Valor' devices, and a Purple Heart. When you told me about Somalia, it seems you were a bit humble in describing your exploits. You're a damn war hero, Joshua. But *look*!" He snatched the sheet up off the table and held it in front of Josh. "No Good Conduct Medals!"

Josh looked at the paper and nodded slightly. "You didn't say what 'egosyntonic' means."

Dorne also nodded slightly, mimicking Josh's behavior. It was time to start laying it on him. The pitch had to come soon. "Egosyntonic is a psychological term referring to behaviors, values, feelings that are in harmony with or acceptable to the needs and goals of the ego, or consistent with one's ideal self-image. It means that your behavior is not at odds with your view of the world. Regardless of whether you are punished for your behaviors in Trait Cluster Zulu, you will continue to exhibit the behaviors because it feeds your sense of right and wrong."

Dorne collected all the papers on the table and placed them in the file folder with his notes. He deliberately closed the folder and put it back in his briefcase. He adjusted his chair closer to the table, folded his hands and leaned over the surface closer to Josh. "Listen," he began, "you can look at your condition in one of any number of ways, but the bottom line is this: You cannot change who you are. If you try and live within this system that is the military, you will break down one way or another. You will languish at mid-grade NCO, Warrant Officer, or Officer. You will continue to see injustice, inefficiency and waste. You will lash out at these, and you will remain in trouble. Or you will swallow yourself and sell out. You'll become numb to the injustice and inefficiency, but you'll still languish in the mid-grades. Either way, you'll be a meaningless cog in a giant clumsy machine. You won't live up to your potential. You won't make a difference. You won't be half the man Lieutenant Colonel Joshua Dante Sabol, III, USMC was."

Josh remained silent, but he was stroking his chin with one hand while his other arm was wrapped around his midsection. When he heard his grandfather's name, he shot a glance at Dorne, but he went on stroking his chin. After 20 seconds of silence, Josh leaned in to Dorne and said, "You're pitching me."

"Of course I am," Dorne replied, not at all shocked that Josh had picked up his tack.

"What are you selling?"

Dorne raised his voice slightly, "I'm not selling a damn thing. I'm telling you there's a way for you to make a difference, but it isn't on your current track."

"What do I have to do?"

Dorne answered without hesitation; "Come with me. Leave everything and don't look back. Now. Tonight."

Josh had stopped stroking his chin. His hands were flat on the table, and his eyes were focused on them. Dorne could tell Josh was struggling with this decision. It must be like a dream for him, Dorne thought. Dorne recalled when he was pitched and how confused he had been. He gave Josh silence to think. Finally, Josh looked up at Dorne and asked, "How do we get out of here?"

Dorne gave Josh a broad smile. "We walk out." He flipped his wrist, looked at his watch then reached inside the suitcase and surveyed the reading on the countdown timer. "We have another 15 minutes before the batteries on this jammer go tits up. You ready?"

"I am."

When Dorne spoke, his Mexican accent was back thicker than ever; "Then let's go. Remember; I'm Flores, and you're in my custody now."

"I'll remember."

"Turns out, I was right after all," said Flores with thickly rolling 'r's'.

"About what?"

"It was your lucky day, cabrone."

0330 HOURS, 29 OCTOBER 1998 – SCHIPHOL INTERNATIONAL AIRPORT, AMSTERDAM, NETHERLANDS

Dorne hadn't said much since they left the Interpol Confinement Facility two hours ago. When Dorne shut the briefcase at the conclusion of the interview, Josh hadn't known what to expect. A shootout and a jail break? Hours of paperwork? Nothing of the sort. Dorne, as Lieutenant Colonel Flores, had obviously arranged for his release prior to speaking with Josh. Flores simply knocked on the interview room door and waited for the guards. When they answered he said, "We're ready," with a thick accent. Two guards escorted Flores and Josh out of the confinement area and into the processing area where Major Tie had dropped Josh a few days ago. Flores signed a single release form, and an Interpol officer gave Josh his personal belongings. At Flores' insistence, they were kind enough to let him keep his Interpol-issued white sneakers and jumpsuit. On the way out the door and into the parking lot, one officer reminded Flores that he was to return Josh into custody within 24 hours. "Sure thing," Flores replied with a smirk and absolutely no accent. He grabbed Josh by the arm and rushed him through the turnstile and into the parking lot. Dorne pointed at a shiny black Mercedes, not unlike the one they had followed a few days prior, and tossed the keys to Josh. "Schiphol," he said when Josh caught the keys.

Now he and Dorne sat near the charter flight line of Schiphol. While Josh drove, Dorne removed his polish with about two dozen wet wipes. When they arrived at the airport, Dorne directed Josh to the far east side of the airport and into the parking area for charter passengers.

Josh's head was swimming with questions. Everything was moving so fast, and Dorne wasn't providing anything close to answers. "I've never been to this side of the airport," Josh said in an effort to get Dorne talking.

"I wouldn't guess that you had," Dorne said as he whipped off the Dress Jacket and threw it in the back seat. "Why don't you get in the back seat, there, and change out of that jumpsuit. There's a duffel bag with a shirt, a jacket and some jeans that should fit you. 34, 34?"

"Close enough," Josh said as he got out of the car and into the back seat. He slipped off the jumpsuit and began to pull the jeans on.

Dorne was changing out of Lieutenant Flores' dress greens in the front seat. "Our flight leaves in about thirty minutes," he said as he pulled a black sweater over his head. "I know you have questions, Josh. Tell you what; you can ask one question. Anything. Shoot."

"Where are we headed?"

"Poland," Dorne answered.

"What's in Poland?"

"Oops," Dorne mocked, "I said one question. Damn, you could have asked anything, and that's what you choose?"

Josh shrugged to himself as he buttoned up the shirt. "It seemed most pressing." Josh held up his arms and the sleeves of the shirt crept up to the middle of his forearm. "What size is this?"

Dorne turned around and looked at Josh. He chuckled and said, "Sorry, kid. I took you for a large. You spend a little more time in the gym than I thought. Just roll up the sleeves and put on the jacket. I didn't pack any shoes as a continuing punishment for those cheap ass loafers you ditched in Luxembourg." He chuckled again.

When Josh finished dressing, he packed his jumpsuit and personal clothes into the duffel bag and zipped it up. He got back in the front seat and exhaled deeply, "Ahhh! Feels better to be out of that thing."

"I bet," Dorne said. He reached into his own duffel in the floorboard and retrieved his trusty laptop. He opened it and checked the screen. Whatever he saw, he seemed satisfied. He slapped the laptop closed and sunk into his own seat, checking his watch. "Twenty minutes." He turned his head and looked at Josh. "You've been a good sport so far, Joshua. I don't know a single recruit who would've come along with so little information. We'll leave that alone, for now. I'll just delude myself and say it's because my pitch was so good."

"It was," Josh said, looking out the windshield at the flight line. A flight crew was finishing fueling and servicing a small 10 passenger Learjet about 50 meters from their Mercedes on the other side of a chain link fence. Josh took another look around the parking lot. It seemed he and Dorne were the only ones waiting, so the Lear must be theirs.

"Yeah right," Dorne said dismissively. "You have no idea what you've gotten yourself into here, but trust me; you made the right decision. Lightning struck and you won the lottery. We both did," he trailed off. He sighed deeply and said, "I haven't slept in four days." He turned his head toward the lights coming off Amsterdam. "You ever hit the Red Light District?"

Josh smiled and turned to Dorne, "Hit it for what?"

Dorne laughed and said, "So much for cyclical conversation." He checked his watch again and closed his eyes.

Two minutes passed. Without opening his eyes, Dorne said, "Look Joshua, this is happening fast for me, too. I'll tell you a few things, because I probably owe you that. First of all, from this point forward things will not slow down for you. Ever. The next three years of your life will be a series of points of instruction, tests and trials. You will be pushed to your physical and mental limits, then past the limits. Then you'll be pushed beyond that. You may not make it through. In fact, you probably will not make it through. Don't concern yourself with that. At all times, you will concern yourself with the task at hand. You will do everything I say until I pass you to someone else. Then you will do everything they say. If at any point, you decide you've had enough, then quit. Of course we both know you won't let yourself quit. If my assessment of you is wrong, you may find yourself in a number of moral quandaries. If you find yourself unable to continue because of your morals and ethics, no offense will be taken and no harm will be done. Just drop out. I don't think my assessment is wrong, though."

"Alright," Josh said.

"Good. The answers to your questions will reveal themselves in time. You may grow impatient, but tough shit. We have a method, and we stick to it for a reason."

"I understand." Joshua thought about asking who the 'we' was, but he decided to keep his questions to a minimum. There would be time for those later.

"No you don't," Dorne said. "You wait. You may not quit, but I promise you that there will be times you'll regret leaving Interpol with me this night. I want you to remember this very moment, sitting in this warm and dry Mercedes when those moments come. Remember this."

"I will," Josh said.

Dorne opened his eyes and checked his watch. "Five minutes. We better get going. Grab the bags out of the back and pop the trunk. I have a few bags back there, too."

Josh grabbed the duffel from the back and walked around behind the vehicle and gathered three suspiciously heavy and unwieldy duffel bags from the trunk. He slung them over his shoulders and turned to Dorne, who was carrying only his own bag.

"Thanks," he said, motioning to the bags on Josh's shoulders. "Toss me the keys."

Josh threw the keys to Dorne. He locked the vehicle and turned toward the gate leading onto the flight line. "Follow me."

They walked to the Lear jet and made their way up the steps and into the plane. It took Josh three trips to load all the bags into the plane. When he finished, Dorne instructed him to pull up the stairs and seal the cabin. He'd never even been on a Learjet, but he figured out the fuselage door quick enough. When he sealed the exterior cabin door, he turned toward the cabin and didn't see Dorne. He could hear noises from the cockpit, so he took a few steps and leaned in. Dorne was sitting at the controls, pushing buttons and checking the systems.

"Where's the pilot?" Josh asked.

"Right here," Dorne said without interrupting his preflight checks. "Take a seat here," Dorne motioned to the co-pilot seat.

Josh sat and watched Dorne go through the systems and power up the plane. As he pressurized the cabin, Dorne turned to him and said, "Put on the headset."

Josh put on the headset and adjusted the mouthpiece.

"We're third in line. Should be about 10 minutes, then we'll taxi to the runway."

"Hey Dorne," Josh said.

"Yeah."

"I didn't see the metal case when I was loading our gear. Where is it?"

"Poland."

1000 HOURS, 29 OCTOBER 1998 – JAROSLAW, SOUTHEAST POLAND

He'd been floating on a hazy cloud of detachment. Kolya knew this sensation well--heroine. In this case, it was probably morphine, straight up. The detached sensation was less pronounced than heroine, but longer lasting with no edge. He had no idea how long he'd been conscious, and he didn't care. He left his eyes closed and ignored that throb in his arm. He mused about the fact that every time he took a breath, the arm seemed to swell and ache. He smiled as he took a deep breath.

Kolya had always been more of a stimulant guy. Cocaine, methamphetamine, PCP, and crack. He enjoyed heroine in Afghanistan, but that was a different time. At first he needed the heroine to dull the edge after a raid. Before Afghanistan, he didn't even drink very much; very odd for a Soviet soldier. During his second tour in the Korengal Valley in Afghanistan, he'd met Oleg. Oleg introduced him to the joys of drug use and taught him how to fight while high. Oleg showed him that alcohol made your aim bad and you couldn't get your cock hard if you were too drunk. Heroine was different, especially when cut with a bit of cocaine--It made the rapes and the executions easier and enjoyable. Kolya smiled and breathed deeply again. He wondered how many bastards he'd fathered in Afghanistan. Hell, how many bastards had he fathered in the world? It took him years to come up with a new method--no need to worry about a bastard if they're dead when you finish with them! The only problem was getting rid of the bodies. He chuckled and breathed deeply, but this time the throbbing in his arm was more pronounced. He still didn't care, but he had a feeling deep in his mind that he soon would.

Who cares, Kolya thought. I'm rich now...wait! His brain was muddled. He tried to put all the events together, but they blended into one another. He remembered the case, Maastricht, cocaine and death metal. But the car was stuck. He'd wait for the buyer, but something happened. What was it? Shattering window and a deafening crack. Then another crack, and another, and another. He'd reached for his AK, but something hit him in the chest. It hit him *hard*. So hard it had knocked him down, then another hard shot in the chest. He heard someone yell, 'Go!', so he tried to get up and go, but he couldn't see and he seized up at the pain in his chest.

Kolya breathed in deeply again, but this time he noticed not only the throbbing in his arm, but also a deep throb in the center of his chest. He kept his eyes closed.

Then he was being dragged out of the house into the mud and snow. He struggled, but something caught him across the bridge of the nose. Kolya crinkled his nose at the thought of the blow, and noticed his face throbbed along with the arm and his chest. The throbbing was becoming distinct.

After the blow to the nose, he felt a prick in his leg. That was it. Where was the case? Where the hell was the case? He tried to take another deep breath, but his chest seized. He tried to reach up to his chest, but his arms wouldn't move. It's time to open your eyes, Kolya thought.

The room was dark, but light was coming in from the crack at the bottom of the door about three meters in front of him. He lolled his head to the side. There was a waist high table built into the wall about two meters to his right. There was something familiar sitting on the table. He squinted his eyes to look at the object, but pure pain shot through his nose. Tears streamed out of his eyes and he tried to reach up to touch his face. He jerked against whatever restraints held his arms, and his whole body erupted in agony. "Uhhhng!" Kolya writhed against the pain and tried to catch his breath.

When the tears cleared, he rested his chin on his throbbing chest and examined his situation. He was seated in a metal chair. There were chains criss-crossing his chest and looped around his lower body and tied to the legs of the chair. Under the chains were ropes. Under the ropes was a white straight jacket. He craned his neck to the right. That arm was behind him. He looked through the chains and the ropes where his left arm was secured tightly to his midsection. Just below the elbow there was a patch of red, and the rest of the sleeve was empty. The shock caused him to jerk against the restraints, which sent another shock of pain through his body. "Uhhhng!"

As the screaming agony withdrew, his vision cleared and he caught a glimpse of the object on the table. The Halliburton case. Next to the case was a stack of file folders, a laptop computer and a Beretta pistol. Between Kolya and the table was a metal tree just over his shoulder. He followed the tree up to an empty plastic bag with tubes descending. He followed the tubes, which led to his right leg. A patch was cut out of his pants where the tubes ended in needles under his skin.

As he gaped at the IV needles, he heard the crunch of tires approaching. Kolya yelled, writhed and cursed against the pain until he passed out.

1115 HOURS, 29 OCTOBER 1998 – JAROSLAW, SOUTHEAST POLAND

They landed at a small international airfield in Rzeszow where yet another Mercedes was waiting for them in the parking lot. Dorne gave the airfield crew instructions to refuel and service the plane. He also filed his next flight plan, but Josh didn't understand a word of Polish. Dorne told Josh to load the heaviest of the duffel bags in the Mercedes.

Josh drove while Dorne pecked away at his laptop. They headed east across large swaths of Polish farmland. Dorne occasionally apologized for the lack of conversation, only saying he had business to attend before their next stop. When they reached the small farm market community of Jaroslaw, Dorne instructed Josh to turn south. They drove another twenty minutes along farm to market roads, going deeper into the rural countryside. When Dorne told him to turn off, Josh didn't even see a road let alone a dirt trail. They continued to drive through what seemed to be a grass field. Josh could see a faint tire trail through the grass, and he followed along the tracks.

"There," Dorne pointed through the windshield at a wooden shack surrounded by trees about 200 meters ahead. Josh drove slowly along the trail, avoiding the rougher muddy patches. When they pulled up to the front of the house, Dorne told Josh to park the vehicle.

Dorne flipped the laptop closed and checked his watch. He grunted to himself and stared at the front door of the shack. "Kolya's in there and so is the case," he said. "You don't speak Russian, do you?"

"No," answered Josh.

"Damn shame," said Dorne, "I have to interrogate this guy and it has to

93

be in Russian. When we go in there, I want you to go to the table on the left and sit down. Don't say a word. There are some files I want you to look through. Most of them are in Russian, but there are plenty of pictures." Dorne looked at his watch again. "His meds should be wearing off about now."

"That was his severed arm, wasn't it?" Josh asked.

"Of course."

"I saw Major Tie Man dig out a silver capsule on the drive to Holland."

Dorne looked at Josh and asked, "'Major Tie Man'?"

"The guy who took me to Interpol in The Hague. The guy whose ass you kicked that night. I named him 'Major Tie Man'."

"Oh yeah," Dorne said, turning back to stare at the door. "We still haven't talked about him. We'll do that after we finish here. I have a lot of questions about that particular man, but they can wait. Anyway, that silver capsule was a tracker. I've seen them before, and I was lucky to catch Kolya's. When I saw those vehicles approaching, I knew something was rotten. When it all went down, I didn't have time to dig out the capsule, so I hacked off the arm just below the elbow."

"How did you know it was in that arm? How did you see them coming? Was that your UAV? How'd you call in that Little Bird? Where did it come from?" Josh asked.

"You ask too many questions," Dorne said. "We'll get to that. You focus on what we're going to do now."

After unlocking the padlock, Dorne walked in and switched on an overhead fluorescent lamp as Josh followed. "Greetings, Kolya!" Dorne yelled in mock warmth. Kolya's head was on his chest, obviously unconscious. "Jesus, he shit himself."

Just as Dorne said it, the reek of feces hit Josh. He shook his head, walked to the table, took a seat and opened the top file. Before he started perusing the files, Josh examined Kolya. Not only had he crapped himself, he'd also urinated. His pants were wet and dripping at the bottom of the cuffs. His bloody stump was wrapped tight around his midsection, but it looked to be oozing through the straight jacket. His nose was badly broken, and his breathing was labored. He was sweating and his entire body was trembling slightly.

"Kolya! Kolya!" Dorne nudged Kolya on the left shoulder. Dorne spat a curse and turned to the table. "Hand me that syringe. The big one."

Josh looked over the Halliburton case at an array of syringes. Most had been used, and he couldn't mistake the one Dorne wanted. It was twice as large as the others and the needle was about three inches long. He grabbed it and handed it to Dorne.

"Adrenaline," Dorne muttered as he took it and popped off the needle cover. He pushed Kolya's head back, slid the needle into his carotid artery and pushed the plunger. He slid the needle out and tossed the syringe over his shoulder. Kolya immediately went into spasms. Josh stood up and looked at Dorne.

"Completely normal," Dorne said as he wheeled a rolling stool in front of Kolya's convulsing body. Dorne casually sat down and measured Kolya's convulsions. Gradually, Kolya's spasms slowed. His breathing relaxed as he regained consciousness. Dorne didn't take his eyes off Kolya as he told Josh to stop gawking and read the files.

Josh started examining the first file, which was all in Russian. As he examined the file, Dorne and Kolya conversed in Russian. Josh could tell from Kolya's tone that he was not fearful. His tone was demeaning, yet Dorne's tone remained calm and even. The file Josh perused was full of pictures of dead bodies, mostly women. Some of the bodies had been dismembered, and all were naked. There were photos of groups of malnourished women in bondage. In another folder, there were photographs of packaged drugs, cash and small arms. Josh surmised this was a file detailing Kolya's crimes. When he reached the folder wherein the reports were in English, most of the papers were stamped 'SECRET' or 'CONFIDENTIAL'. The reports detailed Kolya's history of smuggling narcotics throughout Europe and Asia, trafficking women for prostitution throughout Moldova and the Balkans, smuggling weapons all over the globe, and a patterns of murder and torture of women and rivals. One paper detailed Kolya Aliyev's many arrests by Russian and Interpol authorities. In every case, he had been released after a few days. The longest stretch he'd been incarcerated was six months in Kamchatka, Russia, and that was six years ago. According to the reports, it seemed the Russian Mafia was implicated in securing Aliyev's release on every occasion. When he finished reading through the files, Josh went back to the pictures of dead and dismembered bodies. Five pictures were dated 'October 24, 1998'. There were two female bodies, one blond and one brunette, badly beaten and covered in blood. He laid the photos out and stared at them for a few minutes. He then turned his chair toward the ongoing interrogation.

During the last hour while he was reviewing the files, Josh had heard Kolya say the words 'Yeb t'voy maht' at least a hundred times. He heard the word 'Amerikantsi' about two dozen times from both Kolya and Dorne. Throughout the interrogation, Dorne's voice remained calm and precise. Kolya, on the other hand, was obviously in a good amount of pain. He was sweating profusely, yelling at Dorne and frothing at the mouth. He spit at Dorne a number of times. Dorne simply wiped the spit from his face and continued speaking to Kolya with the same calm tone.

After about 30 minutes, Kolya unleashed a string of what Josh interpreted as curses. He raged against the ropes and chains, and finally spit in Dorne's face again. Dorne sighed, asked Kolya a question to which Kolya responded, "Yeb t'voy maht!"

Dorne stood up and turned to Josh. He shook his head and said, "I'm finished with this guy. He doesn't have anything I need. Your turn. You have any questions for him?"

"No." Josh's eyes hadn't left Kolya, who continued to curse and writhe like an animal.

"Then it's up to you what we do with him," Dorne said.

Josh continued to stare at Aliyev. He turned to Dorne after a moment to find Dorne was standing in the same place, waiting to see what Josh would do. They held one another's eyes for a few seconds. Joshua then pivoted in his stool and grabbed the Beretta. Without hesitation, he took a step toward Kolya, chambered a round, put the weapon to the animal's head and pulled the trigger.

1235 HOURS, 29 OCTOBER 1998 – JAROSLAW, SOUTHEAST POLAND

"Damn!" Dorne yelled as he put his hands up to ears. "As if my hearing wasn't bad enough! A little warning next time!"

"Sorry!" Josh yelled back over the ringing in his own ears. He'd forgotten how loud a gunshot was in an enclosed space.

"Clean that pistol off," Dorne said, still yelling. "And see what you can do about that," he motioned up and down Josh's shirt.

Josh looked at the pistol, then at his shirt. There were bits of flesh, blood and bone spattered across both. He found a rag in a corner table, wet it with some water from the small sink in the opposite corner and cleaned the pistol first. He did his best to clean the shirt, but the damage had been done. He'd have to get rid of the shirt as it had gone from beige to a slight pink.

As Josh tidied himself up, still rubbing his fingers in his ears to allay the ringing, Dorne was gathering the Halliburton case, the laptop and the files on Aliyev. "Alright," Dorne said as he stacked the files, "What do you propose we do with that?" He motioned at Kolya's corpse.

"Bury it?" Josh asked.

"There's already a burn pit out back," Dorne said, scratching his chin. "We'll throw him in there along with a couple of white phosphorus grenades. I have to get rid of the files and the computer, so may as well burn them with the body."

"Won't someone see the smoke?" asked Josh.

"Did you not notice where we are when you were driving out here? Joshua, there isn't anyone out here for miles in every direction. Plus, this is a rural area where people burn their own trash. Didn't you ever burn trash on your granddad's farm? This one," Dorne waved at the corpse, "is no different than anyone else's trash. We'll drag him to the pit and be done with it."

Just as Dorne finished speaking, a giant fart erupted from the corpse. Josh and Dorne looked at the body, then at each other. Dorne laughed first, then Josh joined in. Still giggling, Josh grabbed the back end of the chair and tipped it up as Dorne leaned over and grabbed the legs. Using the chair as a carrier, they hauled the corpse behind the shack and threw it in a shallow pit surrounded by heavy stones.

Dorne instructed Josh to gather some wood to pile on the corpse. While Josh collected wood from around the shack, Dorne went inside and began to wipe down the entire interior of the shack with Lysol, ammonia, bleach, a broom, a mop and damp rags. When Josh had filled the three foot deep pit to the brim with wood, he went inside and helped Dorne scrub the shack.

When they finished three hours later, Dorne sent Josh to the Mercedes to retrieve the sole duffel bag they had brought along. Josh lugged the inordinately heavy duffel, about the weight of a small man, to the fire pit where Dorne was waiting. Dorne unzipped the duffel and began pulling out the contents. First, he retrieved two folding lounge chairs and told Josh to set them up near the pit, but not too close. He then pulled out two small coolers and handed them to Josh with instructions to place them next to the chairs. He pulled out two thermoses and again handed them to Josh. As Josh carried each item to their places next to the chairs, Dorne began stacking items: two Meals Ready to Eat, two white phosphorus grenades, a fifth of Wild Turkey, six bottles of water, two tubes of Pringles, and two sleeping bags rolled tight in stuff sacks. "You want to sleep outside tonight? I know it's cold, but the shack reeks of chemicals."

Josh looked up at the cloudless sky and answered, "Sure."

"We might as well get this going then," said Dorne as he grabbed the first white phosphorous grenade. He walked to the pit and surveyed the pyre. He pulled the pin and dropped the first grenade through the wood and onto Aliyev's chest. The grenade popped and began to sizzle in a high pitched hiss as Dorne turned around to retrieve the second grenade. By the time he returned with the second grenade, nothing remained of the corpse's torso. Shielding his face against the heat, Dorne pulled the pin and dropped the second near what was left of Aliyev's head. They barely heard the pop of the second over the hisses and crackles of the conflagration. They had to move the chairs back a few feet to keep the nylon from melting from the heat of the fire.

"You want the ham slice meal or the beef stew meal?" Dorne asked.

"Beef stew," Josh answered.

"Damn," Dorne spat as he threw Josh the beef stew MRE, "I hate the ham slice."

They sat down and ate their meals while making small talk over the fire. When they finished eating, Dorne opened the first small cooler and pulled out two beers, tossing one to Josh. "Job well done," he said as he cracked the beer. They continued to make small talk and tell jokes while they enjoyed the beers. After his second can, Dorne switched to the Wild Turkey, taking small swigs straight from the bottle. Josh stuck with the beer, supplementing the MRE he'd wolfed down with a tube of Pringles.

The sun was beginning to set and the air was becoming chilly. Josh went to gather more wood and Dorne rearranged the chairs closer to the fire. He found an iron pipe and crushed some of Aliyev's bones that hadn't been melted by the white phosphorous. Josh threw a few pieces of wood on the fire and sat down in his chair, cracking open another beer. They sat in silence for about an hour, watching the fire.

Dorne took a long pull from the bottle and broke the silence; "You must have something you want to talk about."

"I'm trying not to push it," Josh said.

"Go ahead," Dorne said, "Ask."

"Where to begin?" Josh mused. "I guess my main question is; what have I gotten myself into? What is this? Who are you?"

Dorne took another pull off the Wild Turkey. The bottle was half finished. He sighed and said, "I suppose you're due an answer. But I got ahead of myself. First why don't you tell me why you shot Kolya."

"Did I do something wrong?" Josh asked.

"Not at all," Dorne answered. "The desired end state was achieved, but I need to hear a reason."

"You said it was up to me," Josh said. "I weighed out the situation based on what I knew. I also know you left those files there for a reason. You wanted him dead, and I didn't see any need to keep him alive. He was an animal with no intelligence value, nor intrinsic worth as a human being. The world is a better place with him not in it. I'd do it again if I had the opportunity."

Dorne continued to stare into the fire. "It's strange," he said. "To hear someone voice your own thoughts because their mind is so much like your own. I know I made the right choice about you. I could read it in your file, but one can never be sure. A person is not the sum of the parts of their psychological profile. It's dumb luck I happened upon you. I chose to use your team for a number of reasons, but obviously I didn't foresee things going like they did..." He trailed off for a moment then spoke again; "Every time I use military personnel, I do my homework. I pull their files and make sure there's not going to be any trouble. When I pulled your file, I saw you fit a certain profile I've been searching for, and when I saw your outburst in the parking lot, I knew you had to ride with me. Now here we are. But who are 'we' now? That's your question, is it not?"

"I suppose so," Josh answered.

"I'm going to lay some of this out for you, but surely you understand I can't lay it all out. Odds are you will not make it through the phases of your instruction, training and indoctrination. If you do not make it through, or if it turns out I made a mistake about you, we can't have that head of yours full of knowledge about us. Understand?"

"Makes sense," Josh answered.

"We are not affiliated with the military. We are not affiliated or sponsored by any government. We are not contractors. We are not mercenaries. Our mission concerns the National Security of the United States of America. We bring balance, albeit weighted slightly in favor of the United States."

"Balance?" Josh asked.

"You were in the military for a hair over six years. You're very intelligent, and you know as well as anyone the military is a giant lumbering beast incapable of meaningful strategic planning and operations. Sure, they can mount a surgical strike or operation and win a force on force engagement, but the US military is far from the last line of defense."

"What about the CIA?" Josh asked.

"What about them?" Dorne sniffed. "That monstrosity is manned almost exclusively by bureaucratic keystone cops. Too many chiefs, not enough Indians nowadays. They gave us a run in the 1950s and into the 1960s, but they fell apart starting with that Bay of Pigs disaster." Dorne sniffed again and mumbled, "Since then just about everything they've done has been a miniature version of that nonsense."

He took a pull from the bottle, grimaced and continued, "Let me break it down for you on a micro scale for now. You see that?" Dorne pointed at the Halliburton case sitting behind the coolers between their chairs. "No one. Not one soul knew about the contents of that case and where it was heading but us and those assholes who tried to shoot me up. And as you can see, even we didn't know exactly where it was heading. If we hadn't intercepted that case, where would it be now?" Dorne clammed up again for a moment. "That's what we do. We deal exclusively with existential threats to the United States of America. We maintain National Security and stability where others cannot due to self-imposed restraints."

"Restraints?"

"Yes. Restraints," Dorne answered. He took a long pull off the bottle and grimaced when he swallowed. With a hoarse voice he said, "Restraints like the Constitution of the United States of America. That's why you'll renounce you citizenship upon the completion of your instruction, training and preparation."

"What? I'll do *what?*"

"You heard me," Dorne said. He stood up and tossed the empty bottle into the fire. He turned to Josh and asked; "What are you willing to die for?"

Josh looked up at him and replied, "My country. My own country."

"Yes, yes," Dorne waved his hand, "but why?"

"Because it's my home. Unequivocally and objectively, it is the noblest country in the history of mankind."

"But why?" Dorne pressed.

"Liberty," Josh answered. "Freedom. Representative Government. We've created and maintained a near perfect Republic."

"Yes," Dorne said, "and in that Republic there is a social contract guaranteed by the Constitution. In order to preserve that contract, the government must abide by the law. As corrupt as you may believe the US Government is, it still is restrained by the Constitution. The world is a cruel place, seemingly complicated, but simple in nature. A Republic constrained by laws of restrictive self-defense in this world will fall. We ensure it will not. We cannot abide by the same laws that hamstring the US Government. We must have the will to go beyond what is strictly legal in order to preserve the Republic. We cannot do these things while morally and ethically remaining part of the Republic. We take down individuals, groups and regimes using the same tactics and breaking the same laws they would in order to take down the Republic. So we renounce our citizenship and rights afforded to us. We sacrifice what is most important to us, what we would die to protect, in order to ensure the Republic and the liberty it affords its own citizens, lives on and thrives. You cannot do what is required," he motioned into the fire, "and remain a citizen of the United States of America. Surely you understand this concept, Joshua."

Joshua nodded.

Still staring into the fire, Dorne continued, "Let me break it down for you just in case you don't understand exactly what I'm talking about. In one word, describe the Sammies back in Somalia. The ones you fought. The ones you killed." He lolled his head toward Joshua, waiting for an answer.

Josh continued to stare into the blaze. A brief moment later he muttered, "Savages."

"Exactly," Dorne slurred as he turned his gaze back to the fire. "Exactly. They're savages and there are a damn lot more of them out there. More than you can imagine. There are people out there with so much hate and desperation in their hearts that the only thing they want to see is people like us, our friends, our families and our children die. They want to see us burn." He motioned to the case. "If that were a functioning nuke and they found it in their hands, they wouldn't hesitate to put it in the middle of Times Square and set it off. If they had it." Dorne spit in the fire, then continued, "That's where we come in. I'm not just talking about nukes, either. It happens to be my focus, but we're all over the place doing all sorts of crazy shit to make sure the savages who want nothing more than to bring us to our knees never get a whiff of success. So congrats, kid. You actually get to save the world if you can make it through your training and indoctrination and stay alive in the process. No doubt that would make Colonel Sabol very proud."

Josh was no longer staring into the fire. He'd turned his gaze to the dark sky. He was slightly buzzed from the beer, but he fully comprehended the terrifying and sober philosophy Dorne had laid out. He nodded his head and said, "I'm ready."

Dorne grunted and sniffed. "You think so? I was just as excited and ready when my Element laid it out for me."

"Your 'Element'?" Josh asked.

"I'm too drunk," Dorne said, rubbing his forehead. "I'm getting ahead of myself." He staggered to his chair and eased into it. "Ahhh! You know I haven't been drunk in about two years? Of course you didn't know that." He stretched his legs toward the fire. "Where was I? Oh yeah; Elements. That's what we're called, Joshua: Elements. I am Element 65. There are between 100 and 200 Elements at any given time. That's the way it has always been. Each Element must find and recruit their own replacement. If you make it through the training and indoctrination, I believe you'll be Element 120-something. Until then, for the next three years, you'll be referred to as a 'Convert'. If you get through, you'll take my number when I'm finished with this business, making you Element 65. Then hopefully someday you'll find and recruit your own Element. And so it goes."

"How long has this been going on?" Josh asked.

"A very long time," Dorne replied. "Questions like that will be answered in time."

"When do I start my training and indoctrination?" Josh asked.

Dorne grunted and lumbered out of his chair. "Right now." He staggered to the duffel and rummaged through the remaining contents. He pulled out a racquetball and tossed it Josh. "There you go."

Josh caught it and looked back at Dorne, puzzled.

"Work that in either of your hands anytime you're not doing anything else with your hands," Dorne said as he rummaged through the bag. "Squeeze the crap out of it. When it wears out, we'll get you another one. It's for your grip. You have to have a good grip."

"Alright," Josh said as he started squeezing the ball.

"It's a marksmanship thing," Dorne said. He stood up and shambled waving the folding wallet he'd retrieved from the bag in one hand, and a manila envelope in the other. "Here we are," he was starting to slur his words. "Joshua Quinn," he flapped the wallet and the envelope wildly.

"Before I pitched you, I got everything INTERPOL had of yours. You really want to do this? You ready to reverse the course? You want to fade away *and then* burn out?"

Josh smiled and nodded. "I'm ready."

Without ceremony Dorne threw the wallet and the envelope into the fire. He and Joshua watched the envelope catch fire and the leather wallet pucker and bubble. Dorne burped and swayed a bit. "It's not much of a formal procedure or anything. Divers license, military ID, passport, bank card, records pulled from databases, all that. The real work of erasing Joshua Quinn is being done elsewhere. This is more symbolic, I guess." He shuffled back to his chair and eased into it.

They sat in silence for a while, Dorne staring into the fire and Josh squeezing the racquetball and mulling over unanswered and unasked questions. He decided he had nothing to lose by prying at the half drunk Dorne. "Why 'Elements'?"

"Because Joshua D. Quinn no longer exists, Convert," Dorne said as he gazed into the smoldering fire. "Neither does 'Bradley Dorne'. It's only October and I've already been six different people this year. Two more and it'll be a new record. This is something else you'll learn in time." He glanced at Josh, then back at the fire. "Work you grip. Don't make me remind you again."

Josh switched the ball to his left hand, shaking out his right. "How is all this funded?" asked Josh.

Dorne chuckled, "Now *that* is a good question, and one not answered briefly. We'll be leaving in the morning, and we should arrive in New Mexico very early the following morning. The picture will begin to take shape when we get there."

"Alright," Josh said, switching hands again.

"Put it this way," Dorne said as he rose out of his chair, "the contents of that case should fund your entire training. Now," he stretched his arms wide and yawned, "that's it for me."

Dorne grabbed one of the stuff sacks and unpacked the sleeping bag. He laid it out a few feet from the fire and climbed inside. A few minutes later, he was asleep. Josh checked his watch. 0315. Instead of grabbing his own sleeping bag, he continued to work the racquetball and stared up at the sky.

1336 HOURS, 30 OCTOBER 1998 – PORTUGUESE AIRSPACE

"Seventy-two...Seventy-three...Seventy...Four...Seventy...Fff...ive!" Josh brought his knees to the ground and then rolled onto his back panting. Dorne had ordered him to the cabin of the plane to knock out ten sets of 75 push-ups within 30 minutes. Josh looked at his wristwatch. 27 seconds to spare. He got his breathing under control and got to his feet. He retrieved his racquetball from a cabin seat and began working his grip as he made his way back to the cockpit.

"Just in time," Dorne said as Josh eased into the co-pilot seat. "We're making our initial approach into the Azores. I'm going to take you through landing procedures."

"Why are we landing in the Azores?" Josh asked.

Dorne glanced over the instrumentation and made some adjustments as he answered, "First of all, we have to refuel. Second, we're going to pre-clear customs and adjust our flight plan so we can just fly non-stop straight into Albuquerque."

"Is that even possible?" Josh asked.

"Is what even possible? Pre-clearing customs? Refueling? Flying non-stop into New Mexico?" Dorne shook his head at Josh and sighed. "Convert, you need to adjust your sense of what is possible and what isn't possible."

"Understood," Josh answered dutifully.

"I don't think you do, but you will. Let me explain part of it in very simple terms," he motioned toward the cabin where their baggage was stacked. "With a duffel bag full of cash, namely unmarked and nonsequenced one hundred dollar bills, most things in the civilized world are possible. Remember that."

"I will," Josh said.

Dorne nodded his head. "Good. Now you see that display there? That's your artificial horizon. As we're coming in, you'll want to make sure you keep those little white wings in there between the blue and the brown. This display here is your airspeed, which is probably the most important thing when you're landing...."

Dorne went on to explain in detail every aspect of landing the Gulfstream. At 40 kilometers from the airfield, he let Joshua take the yoke and control the approach for about a minute. Once they landed, Dorne taxied down the small runway toward the fuel point, all the while speaking to the tower first in very formal and professional English. After the English formalities, Dorne switched to what Josh surmised was Portuguese. While speaking Portuguese, Dorne's tone was playful and joking. Although Josh couldn't understand a word spoken, it seemed as if Dorne and the man with whom he was speaking in the control tower had known one another since childhood. Once at the fuel point, Dorne took off his headset and went back to the cabin to let down the ramp. He unzipped one of the duffel bags and began transferring stacks of US dollars wrapped in plastic to a small paper grocery sack. When he had loaded the grocery sack half full of cash, he wadded the top and tossed it to Josh.

"Hold that. Customs will be here any minute. When they get here, they'll give me a stack of papers. When I take the papers, you toss them the sack. Don't say a word." Josh could plainly see Dorne was giddy. He loved every minute of this. He was like a 12 year old tagging his first rail car all the while knowing, *knowing*, he'd get away with it.

While they waited, a fuel crew got busy refueling the plane. About the same time they coupled the fuel lines to the plane, a Portuguese Customs vehicle approached the plane and parked near the nose. Two uniformed agents, one grossly overweight and one abnormally tall and skinny, exited the vehicle and made their way to the stairs. As they approached the ramp, Dorne leaned out of the fuselage and yelled, "O que e novo, porcos?" The men both answered with laughter and greeted Dorne as they made their way up the steps and into the cabin. Once inside, the fat man and Dorne exchanged jokes and arm punches while the tall man briefly scanned the cabin. Neither seemed to notice Josh existed, but when the tall man was scanning the cabin, his eyes stopped for a moment on the grocery sack in Josh's right hand. When the tall skinny man was satisfied with his scan, he whipped out a small clipboard and began signing pieces of paper, occasionally chuckling at something Dorne had said to the fat man. The tall guy stacked his signed papers and shouldered over to Dorne, handing him the stack. He then turned toward Josh. Josh met his eyes for a moment, then remembered his role. He tossed the grocery sack to the tall man. He caught the bag in one hand, pivoted, slapped the fat man on the back, said something in Portuguese, and exited the aircraft. The fat man and Dorne exchanged one last joke and then the fat guy waddled his way down the ramp and back to their vehicle.

"Too easy," Dorne said as he gave a last wave to the Portuguese Customs officers. He then retracted the ramp and nudged past Josh and into the cockpit. "They should be done fueling in about 10. Join me up here and I'll walk you through the take off."

As promised, Dorne guided Josh through the take off and then allowed him to take the Gulfstream to cruising altitude. Once there, Dorne sent Josh back to the cabin to repeat the ten sets of 75 push-ups within 30 minutes. This time, Josh met the deadline with only five seconds to spare. He wiped the sweat from his face and neck with his shirt, picked up his racquetball and huffed his way back into the cockpit. Dorne was leaning far back in his seat, pecking away at the laptop as usual.

As soon as Josh settled in the seat, Dorne asked, "Did you cheat?"

"No," Josh answered.

"So your form was perfect on every repetition?"

"No. But I did knock out ten sets of legitimate push-ups."

"Good answer," Dorne said. He slapped the laptop closed and checked the gauges in front of him. "I'll give you an hour rest, then you'll repeat the drill. Understood?"

Josh nodded and stared out the window, working the racquetball in his left hand.

Dorne popped his knuckles and let out a big sigh. He regarded Joshua for a moment then asked, "You're really all-in for this, aren't you?"

Joshua didn't break his stare out the window and said, "Yes. Why? Is there something I'm doing that's wrong?"

"Not at all," Dorne answered. "You're just a little less questioning than I was with my Element."

Josh turned back to Dorne and said, "I suppose I figure everything will be revealed in time. I understand your need to limit my knowledgeability. Need to know, and all that."

"I get it," said Dorne. "I just hope you're ready for the next couple of years. I don't know if I stressed that enough last night in Poland. Let me stress it again now while we're both completely sober: the next 18 to 30 months is a series of tests. I'm not talking about the physical tests, although you will go through more physical pain and suffering than you've ever experienced. It isn't enough to be physically strong to do what we do. I'm talking about the mental and spiritual toll the training and this way of life will take on you. It's true that you're an 'Egosyntonic Axis IV Sociopath', but many times this 'gift', as we call it, isn't enough to counter the stress put on your psyche. You'll very soon learn that we operate in a manner that will brutally try every idea you have or have ever had about right and wrong. As you can imagine, not everything is as black and white as that piece of shit Russian you aerated back at that farmhouse in Poland. You must come to terms that the ends justify the means, whatever those means may be. If at any time you can no longer handle the means, just quit. Don't force yourself to stick with it just because you've never quit anything in your life. This is completely voluntary, and you're hurting us and yourself if you're not totally committed."

"What happens if I quit?" asked Josh.

"You'll disappear," Dorne answered.

Josh stopped working the racquetball.

Dorne shook his head and smiled. "Not in that way. We'll take care of you. We'll set you up. But you will have no choice but to live a life in no way associated with any level of the government or military. I'm sorry, but that's what you've signed on to. But we'll worry about that only if we have to worry about it."

Dorne leaned forward and checked the readings on the panel above his head. He leaned back down in his seat and said, "I'm not wrong about you, Joshua. You're the one I've been waiting for. You'll make it."

"Thanks," Josh said.

"Don't thank me for this," Dorne said. "You'll learn to curse my name for doing this to you. It happened to me and every Element I know. It will be the day you look in the mirror and realize you no longer know who you are or where you came from. You just have to keep the faith. Not in me, but in the true cause we serve. I'm not wrong about you. There's a storm coming. You're going to make it and we need you."

1945 HOURS, 30 OCTOBER 1998 – TBILISI, GEORGIA

"Mr. Goldstein," said a voice over the desktop intercom, "another call for you from the Paris Station. Should I take a message?"

Noah sighed and pressed the intercom button, "No, Mandy. I'll take it. Thank you."

He picked up the phone and pressed the blinking button. "What is it, Stanley? This is the fourth call in as many hours. I shouldn't even be at work right now."

"Level with me, Noah," said the voice on the other end, " What do you know about this mess I've been cleaning up for the last three days?"

"I've been reading the cables," Noah answered. "What makes you think I have anything to do with that fiasco, Stanley? What was that, by the way?" Noah took off his bifocals and rubbed between his eyes.

"If you've been reading the cables, you know as much as we know," Stanley replied, "but some of the records off those dead bodies are being traced to the Caucasus region, and you're the man in your region. Everything goes through you and from what I know, very little gets by you. So if you know anything, you need to let me know now. Heads are gonna start rolling soon. Firefights, napalm and burned bodies don't go over well in the Western European countryside. If I don't come up with some answers and damage control soon, we're cooked. Thank God the press hasn't caught wind of this yet." Noah leaned back in his chair, still rubbing his eyes. "You think they will catch wind of it?"

"Naw," Stanley said. "We've paid the right people to keep quiet, but that doesn't guarantee anything, as you well know."

"Look Stanley," Noah sighed, "I don't know anything, and even if I did I wouldn't tell you about it. I'm about a month from retirement, and I'm not risking shit."

"Damn you, Noah. Any bone you can throw me..."

Mandy came over the intercom again, "Mr. Goldstein, you have a visitor. He says he needs to see you immediately."

Noah cupped a hand over the phone and yelled, "Mandy! Who is it?"

"He says his name is James Bu...Sir! Sir! You can't just walk--" just as the intercom went dead, Noah could hear Mandy's voice in the hall. "Mr. Butler! Mr. Butler! Please, sir, you need an appointment!"

"Stanley, I'm going to have to talk to you later," Noah said as he hung up the phone. Noah could hear Stanley's protestations as the handset hit the receiver.

Mandy had managed to get in front of the man and entered Noah's office barely before him. "Mr. Goldstein, I'm very sorry," she said in a huff, "but this man," she motioned at the door as the man entered the room.

"That's alright, Mandy," Noah said as he put his glasses back on and rose out of his chair with a grunt. "Please excuse us and close the door on your way out."

The immaculately dressed man swept past Mandy and tossed a thick leather business satchel down on the couch beside Noah's desk. He then shot his cuffs and seated himself next to it. Mandy gave him an incredulous look and backed out of the room with a scowl. "Yes, sir," she said as she closed the door.

"So," Noah began as he plopped back down into his leather chair, "you certainly made a hash of things, didn't you?"

"I'm here to fix that," the man said. He motioned to a thick leather business satchel he had thrown on the couch as he had sat down. "We appreciate your help with this matter, we're nearly done with you."

"Thank God for that," Noah said. "You've been nothing but a pain in the balls since you first darkened our door here. In all my thirty five years with the Agency, I've never seen anything like this."

"Really?" the man asked.

"Yes really." Noah answered. "A snot nosed major walks in and gets to give *me* orders. *I'm* the Chief of Station. *I* call all the shots. It's a different Agency when Department of Defense calls the shots, I suppose."

"Who said I was Department of Defense?" asked the man.

"*Major* James Butler," Noah said snidely. "*Major*. DoD are the only ones who use ranks like that. Plus, you carry yourself like a soldier."

"I am a soldier," Butler said, "but I don't work for DoD. I've been tasked to work for a new Department within the Federal Government. We don't have a name yet, but I imagine the word 'homeland' will be part of the title someday. I'm surprised you didn't bring up these points when you signed over 8.7 kilograms of refined plutonium."

"I was told not to ask questions," Noah said. "I'm only a month from retirement. I don't want anything to get in the way of that. When I signed that over to you, I had no idea what it was for, and I still don't. I don't give a shit. You told me I'd get it back the next time I saw you, and here you are. Judging from that satchel, you do not have the ring with you."

"I do not," Butler said. "That plutonium ring is gone for the foreseeable future."

Noah took off his bifocals again and buried his face in his hands. He groaned and said, "You bastard. You realize the position in which you've put me?"

"I do," Butler said evenly. "I understand the plutonium ring was on loan from the Georgians?"

"Yes," Noah said through his hands. "I pulled all sorts of strings to get that plutonium ring. I made every promise and called in every favor. I was going to retire here in Tbilisi. When I tell them they're not getting that ring back, I'll be standing tall in front of president Shevardnadze within a week signing persona non grata paperwork."

"I doubt that," Butler said.

Noah lifted his head and looked at Butler. "What planet do you live on?"

Butler took the satchel and put it on Noah's desk. "In this satchel is 100 million dollars in bearer bonds. That should be more than enough to get this situation under control and keep it quiet. Hell, it's enough to buy 16 kilograms of plutonium. You should have enough left over to upgrade whatever dacha in the Georgian countryside in which you plan to retire."

Relief swept over Noah as he opened the satchel and flipped through the stack of bearer bonds. In this part of world, money solved every problem, even a problem of missing plutonium. He'd be able to pay off his assets who had lent him the plutonium, along with any member of the Georgian government who might have knowledge of the transaction. And Butler was right--there'd still be plenty left over for him. The retirement package the Agency provided wouldn't be quite enough to allow him to live at a level of comfort commensurate with his efforts over the last 35 years.

"All is well?" Butler asked.

"Oh yes," Noah sank back into his chair. "All is well. I can cover this fairly easily."

"So we're in the clear?"

"Sure," Noah said.

"Good," said Butler. "Now I have a few questions."

"Such as?"

"How can I track that plutonium ring?"

"Track it?" It hadn't occurred to Noah that the good Major might have actually lost the ring. "Why would you need to track it?"

"Just answer my question," Butler said.

"I can't answer unless you tell me who has control of the ring, or at least what you think they plan to do with it. Unless you tell me some specifics, we'll be here all night with me explaining an infinite number of possibilities."

Butler sat for a moment contemplating what to say next. After a few moments, he cleared his throat and said; "Let's just say I have a feeling the ring will be taken back to the States. How can I track it?"

"Well," Noah began, "First of all, I'm no nuclear physicist. I have, however, worked a few operations dealing with nuclear arms and components. Just keep in mind my knowledge is just above that of layman."

"Understood," Butler said. "Go on."

Noah nodded and pushed up his bifocals, "I don't know exactly where this particular plutonium originated, but since it isn't spherical, I'm assuming it was refined at a former Soviet nuclear power plant for use as a power source rather than for a weapon. That isn't to say it can't be weaponized, it would just be very difficult."

"Alright," Major Butler shifted in the couch.

"Yes," Noah continued, "how to track it. I'm assuming you don't have positive control of the item."

Butler looked at the ceiling and shook his head. "Go ahead and assume that."

Noah nodded his head and said, "So somewhere in the States we have a plutonium 239 ring made in Russia. If the party that has control of the ring wants to sit on it, you won't be able to track it unless they're fool enough to leave it in the open without shielding. If they have the most rudimentary lead lining, that would suffice to throw off any radiation detector. Is it already through customs?"

"Assume it is," Butler said.

"Right," Noah continued, "now if the controlling party wishes to part with the ring, you'll have your chance to track it. The controlling party will try to sell the plutonium ring to any number of nuclear laboratories in the States or Canada. The Department of Energy has a fairly robust tracking system when it comes to radioactive material like plutonium 239 and 238. If the plutonium was spherical, you could pick it up a few days after the potential sale of the item. There aren't many plutonium spheres on the planet, and they're usually sitting on the tip of an ICBM. They're very unstable, as well. Even a small mistake in handling the sphere could cause a criticality."

Butler shook his head and said sarcastically, "Good thing it isn't a sphere, then."

Noah nodded. "I apologize for the digression. I'm just trying to think this out." Noah leaned back in his chair and gazed at the ceiling, pondering the question and the possible answers. After a few moments and still gazing at the ceiling, he began to speak again. "You haven't given me very much information about the controlling party and based on our interactions thus far, I am assuming you will not be giving me further information. That makes it difficult for me to give you a complete picture," he broke his ceiling gaze to glance at the satchel of bearer bonds. "But I'll give it a shot. The only viable option is to track the plutonium through sale. The sale of this ring hinges on its purity. If terrorists or rogue states are buying it, they won't take less than ultra-purified weapons grade. The only party interested in semi-pure fuel grade or reactor grade plutonium would be the US government, and the controlling party wouldn't be fool enough to try to sell to them. My recommendation is to monitor chatter to and from rogue states and try to monitor the outgoing ports, particularly to North Korea, Iran, and Iraq. Closely monitor any off shore cash transactions between 40 and 60 million dollars."Noah hadn't noticed Butler was inspecting his fingernails with a pointed disinterest in any of Noah's recommendations. Butler interrupted Noah's pontifications with a loud throat clearing. Noah took his eyes off the ceiling and looked at Butler.

"Well thank you very much," Butler said while brushing one fingernail with the tip of his thumb, "for nothing. To think I believed the a washed up Station Chief who's retired on duty would have anything meaningful to add was a mistake, and one I'm not likely to repeat."

Noah gaped as Butler stood. He continued, "I should have left that," he motioned at the satchel, "back in Western Europe and let you figure this shit out yourself. You see you're not, nor have you ever been, in the fight. You and all your Cold Warrior ladder climbers in almost every Embassy in the world--It's time for you to step aside. You're very lucky you're only a month away from retirement, or I'd have your job, you fat piece of shit." Butler straightened his tie and turned to make his way out of the office. "This may be your country, but this is my world. Have a nice life. If you breathe a word about me or this operation to anyone, ever, then to me that means you've chosen to die in your sleep very soon after." Butler turned briskly and walked out of the office.

Noah heard a door slam down the hall. He tried to be outraged, but he realized he didn't disagree with anything Butler had said. He sighed and lumbered out of his chair and around to the couch. He picked up the satchel, set it on the coffee table, and began counting the bearer bonds. He laid them in three neat piles: assets, payoffs, and retirement.

0900 HOURS, 1 NOVEMBER 1998 – ALBEQUERQUE, NEW MEXICO

Somewhere over Virginia, Josh lost count of how many sets of push-ups he'd done. After every set, he'd come huffing back into the cockpit, only to sit for about twenty minutes before Dorne sent him back to the cabin to knock out another 10 sets of 75. Around Josh's sixth trip to the cabin, Dorne told Josh this new push-up regimen was to become a daily requirement in addition to the non-stop fiddling with the racquetball. No less than 1500 push-ups daily, no matter what.

Over Missouri Dorne sent Josh to the cabin, not to knock out another set of push-ups, but to wrap the Halliburton case in thick lead-lined blankets. Josh took the blankets out of the heavy duffel, noting their close resemblance to the thick X-ray blankets at the dentist's office, and wrapped the case. He then took a roll of duct tape from the duffel and completely covered the case and blankets in a thick coat of gray tape as per Dorne's instructions.

On the approach to Albuquerque International Sunport, Dorne allowed Josh to guide the Gulfstream through the entire approach, although Dorne took the controls as they made their landing. They taxied into the charter area where Josh unceremoniously unloaded their cargo, including the unwieldy Halliburton case which was now nothing more than a clump of lead-lined blankets and tape.

Josh loitered with the cargo while Dorne retrieved their waiting vehicle-- a black Mercedes Sport Utility Vehicle. Josh shook his head as Dorne screeched to a stop next to the pile of duffels. As they loaded their cargo, Josh looked around as if at any moment some unnamed authority would roll up on their elicit operation.

Sensing Josh's apprehension Dorne said, "What the hell are you looking around for? You look like a damn criminal. Didn't I tell you? We settled in Portugal for about 60 grand, my friend. We're wired tight. As always. Damn! Now load that case in the back seat where I can see it."

Josh nodded and continued to load.

After settling their parking fee with the charter terminal, Dorne took Interstate 25 north to a Brooks Brothers factory store. Upon seeing the store closed until noon since it was a Sunday, Dorne pulled out his computer and tapped away for a few moments. Finding the information he needed, he slapped the case closed then dug around in one of the duffels. He pulled out a cellular phone and dialed a number while squinting at the screen. He held then phone up to his ear and rubbed his eyes. When he heard a voice on the other end he violently shook his head free of the cobwebs of a trans-Atlantic flight and exclaimed, "Jimmy! Did I wake you? 'Course not, 'course not. It's Randy...yeah, *that* Randy. I got an emergency, here. I have a buddy who's got a job interview today...yeah today...yeah, yeah I know it's Sunday...can you do me a solid and come up here and open this place up? My pal needs to be measured up...Jimmy, Jimmy, Jimmy! Yeah, Jimmy. The usual...hey man, I can always take my business somewhere else...yeah...that's what I thought. I'm parked out front, and get here quick. His interview is just after noon, every minute you waste is a Benjamin less than usual." He ended the call and exhaled, "You gotta love the private sector. He'll be here in ten."

Fifteen minutes later, Josh was in his underwear standing on a small wooden box in front of a mirror. Jimmy, a squirrelly man in his early twenties dressed in a track suit was taking his every measurement with a tape while Dorne chatted up the fidgety little man about the latest news concerning the Los Angeles Dodger's minor league team, the Albuquerque Isotopes. Once the measurements were finished, Jimmy disappeared into the stock room. Thirty minutes later, Jimmy emerged with a charcoal gray pinstriped suit on a hangar.

Dorne shook his finger and said, "Oh no, Jimmy. Two shirts, two ties, two pairs of socks and a pair of shoes, and make sure they all match. I want to get my money's worth today. And throw in one of those fancy wrist watches I read so much about in Gentleman's Quarterly."

Jimmy shrugged and disappeared into the stock room and later emerged with the requested products. Dorne motioned Josh over to Jimmy and said, "Suit up, son."

Josh obliged and stepped into the changing room. Moments later, he came out fully dressed in time to see Dorne, who had also changed into a clean suit, handing Jimmy a thick envelope.

"Until next time, Jimbo," Dorne said. "Now unlock this door. We have an interview to get to."

Dorne took Interstate 25 north to Interstate 40 east. As he drove, he outlined Joshua's instructions for the meeting. They were going to meet Bobby Truman, a years-long business partner of Dorne's. Bobby dropped out of MIT in the middle of his sophomore year and struck out on his own. He was a Renaissance Man, of sorts: nuclear physicist, mechanical engineer, and entrepreneur. Bobby had patented and sold numerous heat shield designs to NASA as well as designing and selling components to mass spectrometers to almost every laboratory with a Nobel Prize winning physicist or chemist. Bobby amassed $350 million through his ventures, but he never did any of this for the money.

"Why does he do it?" Josh asked.

"He has a chip on his shoulder. He sees his peers who graduated MIT and Harvard working at these labs, getting their tenures and winning awards and he knows he's smarter than any of them. He wants to prove he's better than them, but he doesn't want to prove it to the world--he needs to prove it to himself. That's why I know I can trust him. I provide him with resources to further his research and business ventures. He doesn't ask questions, and he pays cash. Over the last two years, Bobby has been tinkering with all things atomic--medical devices, efficient thermodynamic transport, advanced reactor design, focused ion beams, weapon design, and so on. I think you understand why we're on our way to see him today."

"Weapon design?" Josh asked.

"Theoretical stuff," Dorne answered. "Nothing to worry about."

Josh nodded and asked, "And who are you to this man? Who am I? What's the protocol, here?"

"I'm a business man and he doesn't care who my employer may be. He never asks questions about that, but I ask questions as to his intentions with the products I am selling as well as his wish list of products he desires to purchase. Look at it this way--our relationship is more like that of a pawn shop. You? You're simply my associate. Keep your mouth shut if you're not absolutely sure of what you want to say. Bobby Truman is one of the most intelligent men you'll meet in your life, and he does not suffer fools or jack-ass questions."

Joshua flashed his eyebrows up and shrugged slightly.

"I saw that," Dorne said as he exited the interstate. "What's the problem?"

"This is a lot to take in," Josh answered. "Security wise."

Dorne shook his head. "Look, we don't have enough time for me to explain the relationship Bobby and I have developed. I don't have time to allay your fears about my operational security. I'd hoped after witnessing the events of the last nine days, I'd have built up a little credibility in your mind--"

"You have, but..."

"Mm-hm," Dorne waved his hand, "save it. It's is a lot to take in." Dorne turned off the interstate access road and onto a side street. "I've been doing this for over seven years and whoever you're afraid of has never so much as sniffed me...." Dorne paused, then continued, "Until the other night. And you saw how that turned out. We don't fail, Convert."

Dorne turned off the side street and pulled into a short drive way and stopped at a chain-link gate. He gave three honks and leaned over the steering wheel, presenting his face to a camera mounted on the top of the gate's pole. After a moment he leaned back into the seat, sighed and rubbed his eyes again. The gate then opened and Dorne pulled into a driveway to the front of a single story windowless concrete building about the size of small grocery store. Dorne stopped at the solitary doorway leading inside the building.

"Here we are," Dorne said as he opened the door. He then pulled his leg back in the vehicle and shut the door. "One more thing, Convert. Bobby Truman is completely blind."

"Then what's with the suits?" Josh asked.

"He'll smell them and appreciate the fact we went to the effort." Dorne answered as he opened the SUV door again and stepped out. "Grab the case and let's go inside."

Joshua retrieved the bulky lead wrapped case from the back seat and followed Dorne to the door. To Joshua's surprise, Dorne simply opened the metal door and sauntered inside as Josh followed. They were greeted by an attractive blond receptionist sitting behind a desk.

Dorne bowed in mock formality to the woman and said, "And hello, hello, hello Miss Tessa Woodward! You look as lovely as ever!"

Tessa's face lit up as she rose, pulled down her rather short skirt and made her way around the desk to Dorne, "And hello to you," she said.

Before she reached him, obviously going in for a hug, Dorne grabbed her hand and dropped to one knee. He made a show of kissing her hand, and he slowly rose still holding her fingers. "Ah, ah, ah," he said mockingly. "It would be unprofessional of me to display public affection, Miss Woodward."

"This evening then, Mr. Randal McNeill?" she asked with a heavy flirtatious tone. Joshua made note of that. Dorne, or Element 65, is now 'Randal McNeill."

"Of course!" Randal answered as he stepped back and admired her, still holding her hand. "The usual, Miss Woodward. Dinner at six. You bring the massage oil. Bring extra, because I need it."

Miss Woodward cocked her head to the side as she stepped close to Randal and slightly pushed her considerably large breasts into his chest. Randal simply smiled and cocked his head, as well. Satisfied, she turned to make her way back around the desk, but not before Randal slapped her right butt cheek. She giggled as she rounded the desk. Randal turned to Josh and winked with a mischievous smile. She hadn't seemed to notice Josh through all the flirtations and sexual tension.

Tessa Woodward picked up the phone and said, "Mr. Truman, sir? Two visitors, full access. Yes, sir."

She motioned Joshua and Randal McNeill to a heavy steel door to their right. Randal walked to the door and Josh followed. The sound of powerful servos filled the reception area as the 12 inch thick steel door slowly swung open. Randal and Josh stepped in and walked down a narrow hall as the door swung closed behind them. The temperature dropped considerably as they made their way down the long hall. Josh hadn't noticed the sweat dripping down his back from holding the unwieldy lead wrapped Halliburton case until now, as the chill made its way through his suit. When they reached the end of the hall, Randal turned right into a massive laboratory workspace.

"Bobby!" Randal yelled as he entered the massive room. "Bobby! It's Randy!"

"Over here," Josh heard someone say as he rounded the corner into the laboratory.

In the far left front corner of the lab stood a tall thin man assembling what looked to be a electric generator. He was the only person in the room except Josh and Randal. As Randal made his way to the man, who was obviously Bobby Truman, he didn't pause in assembling the generator. He was staring wide-eyed into space as his hands meticulously worked. Bobby then spoke as Randal approached, "*Randal*. We both know that's not your name, so don't patronize me. You can fool that Bimbo out front, but not me."

Randal McNeill chuckled and shook his head. He seated himself across the workbench where Bobby was assembling the generator. "Alright," he said, "let me have it."

Still staring wide-eyed, Bobby grabbed a screwdriver then took a deep sniff. "Brooks Brothers again. Very nice. What color?"

"Black," answered Randal.

"Black," repeated Bobby. "What's the occasion?"

"Just came in to talk business with you, Bobby."

"I see," Bobby said curtly as he turned the screwdriver furiously. He put the screwdriver to the side and grabbed another tool Joshua didn't recognize. "Who is this with you?"

"My associate," Dorne answered. The smile on Randal's face hadn't faded. This was their usual banter. "He's the reason we're here."

Bobby was now using the tool, which was some sort of gauge, to measure the circumference of the rotary converters. Without pausing his work, he began to berate Randal and Josh, "What is it this time, *Randal Mcneill?* Cesium-137 pellets? A fully assembled MIRV-6 warhead? An infrared nose cone of a GBU? You think I'll just buy the crap you bring in here because it's rare? I have a business to run, *Randal.*"

Randal McNeill held his smile and turned to Josh. "Mr. Akkerman? Please explain what we have for Mr. Truman." Randal McNeill turned back to Bobby and motioned to Josh, "Bobby Truman, Sean Akkerman."

Josh took note, 'Sean Akkerman'. Where did that come from?

Bobby continued making measurements and feeling the results, still staring off in the same space. "So, *Sean Akkerman,*" his voice was dripping with derision at the name, "what do you have for me?"

Sean cleared his throat and looked at the lead wrapped case. He heaved the case onto the work station and set it next to the generator. "I have approximately eight kilograms of plutonium 239."

Bobby paused for an almost imperceptible moment, turned his wide eyes slightly toward the case, then continued reading his measurements with his finger. "We'll see about that," he said with doubt in his voice. He set the measuring tool to the side and made his way around the table. He walked toward the rear of the lab, nimbly avoiding lab chairs and equipment. He said over his shoulder, "Follow me, gentlemen. Bring that case you have wrapped in dental protective blankets." Sean noticed a bit less derision in Bobby's tone.

The far rear left corner of the lab was a mass of spectrometers connected to computer stations and server trees. Bobby stopped at the largest spectrometer machine and instructed Sean Akkerman to strip the case of the lead blankets. After cutting the blankets away, Bobby instructed Sean to place the case inside a compartment within the spectrometer. Sean obliged as Bobby shut the glass door and keyed a number of commands on the spectrometers console. A printer behind Bobby immediately whirred to life and began spitting out small sheets. Bobby took all three sheets and ran his fingers over them. Amazed at the technology of a Braille printer, Sean looked over at Randal. Randal was still smiling. He nodded his head at Sean, then raised his eyebrows and nodded at Bobby Truman as if to say, 'told you he was intelligent'.

"Good," Bobby said as his fingers finished the last sheet. "Now, pull the case out and open it." Sean lifted the glass, pulled out the case and set it on the table. He snapped it open and lifted the lid.

"Tell me what you see," Bobby instructed.

Sean described what he saw: a small ring of metal sitting in the middle of black foam casing. It was rough and unpolished. The ring was dull gray with slight bronze streaks, and about the size of a cut piece of PVC plumbing pipe.

"It's a ring," Bobby said.

"It is," Sean answered.

"That may affect the price I'm willing to pay," Bobby said as he stroked his chin. His wide eyed gaze was again fixed in space. "But I get ahead of myself. Grab those plastic tongs." He motioned to the table behind Sean. "Take the ring out of the case and place it back in the spectrometer."

As Sean obliged, Bobby returned to the control panel and tapped a few commands. Again, the printer spat out three sheets of Braille. Bobby perused the information with his fingers, then set the papers aside. He shook his head and the corner of his mouth curled in the slightest smile, his eyes never leaving that point in space.

"I have good news and bad news," he said.

Randal spoke for the first time in almost half an hour, "Please explain in detail." His eyes shot to Sean and he
winked.

"Gladly," Bobby said. He began to pace the area around the spectrometer. He turned his wide eyes to the floor as he began his dissertation. He spoke as if he were lecturing first year junior college students. "When you gentlemen *acquired* this ring, I imagine you thought you were carrying ultra pure weapons grade plutonium-239. You thought old Robert Compton Truman would want to buy your ultra pure plutonium. The problem, gentlemen, is that I have no use for ultra pure plutonium-239. I have no desire to build a Teller-Ulam thermonuclear weapon, which is the only thing ultra pure plutonium-239 is good for. The good news for you is that this ring grades out at just below what is called 'ultra high'. I can use this and I wish to purchase it from you. 45 million."

Randal clapped his hands abruptly and held them over his head as if signaling a touchdown.

Sean Akkerman shook his head.

"What seems to be the problem, Mr. Akkerman?" Bobby asked.

Sean answered, "I'm afraid I do business a little differently than my associate, Mr. Truman."

Randal brought his hands down and folded them behind his head. He rolled his eyes, leaned back in his chair as if settling in for a long, boring debate.

"Before I agree to sell this item to you," Sean began, "I require an explanation as to its intended use."

"Since when does the seller require an explanation?" Bobby asked. Sean could tell Bobby wanted to explain the intended use.

"Since you started doing business with me," Sean shot back. "I'm not a nuclear physicist. I'm nowhere near that smart. But my friend, I am smart enough to know that I shouldn't agree to a price of something I'm selling without knowing the value of that item. I require an explanation."

Out of the corner of his eye, Sean saw Randal shrug slightly and nod his head in agreement.

Josh continued, "Mr. Truman, you obviously know my associate and I are more than simple businessmen. Mr. McNeill may not have informed you thus far throughout the course of your business relationship as to specific concerns we may have as to the products we've sold you in the past. I am here to inform you. From this point forward, we will require a verbal synopsis of the product's intended use. Agreed?"

Bobby hadn't shifted his blind stare from the far corner of the lab, but he had turned his head to hear every word Sean spoke. He tilted his head and asked, "If I don't agree?"

"We'll take our business elsewhere," Sean answered.

"You have other clients?" asked Bobby.

Sean turned to Randal and answered, "We do." Randal shook his head in frustration. "But we prefer," Sean said, "to maintain our relationship with a scientist of your renown. Simply put, Mr. Truman, we admire your work. But in the end, this is a business venture. We've seen your end products are extremely successful, and we see that our profit margins would be significantly higher if we might invest in your end products produced from the items we regularly sell you."

Randal was thoroughly perplexed. He held his hands up as if to ask, 'what the hell?' Sean simply nodded his head toward Bobby Truman. Randal looked and saw Bobby nodding his head.

"Investors," Bobby said.

"Yes," answered Sean.

"I agree," Bobby said, "but you must sell the plutonium ring to me for 30 percent less than asking price, and you will take two percent profit on the finished product."

Sean countered, "We need an explanation as to the intended use before we agree to percentages."

"Fair enough," Bobby said. He shifted his stare to the floor and began pacing as he outlined the intended use. "I plan to use this plutonium as the fuel for a radioisotope thermoelectric generator which will power a deep space probe. A contractor employed by JAXA, the Japan Aerospace Exploration Agency, has sub-contracted me to build this generator."

"What is the end price?" Sean asked.

"It's a blind contract," Bobby answered as he continued to pace, "pardon the pun. They have no idea what this will cost, so I will name my price once the generator proves functional. I was planning on trying to acquire plutonium-238, which would have powered the generator for 23 years. Plutonium-239 of the purity you've provided will extend the life of my generator by at least 80 years."

"What is the purpose of the probe?" Sean asked.

Bobby laughed as he paced, then answered, "That's the beauty of this contract. The Japanese are forward looking people, sometimes to their financial detriment. The Metal Mining Agency of Japan has partnered with JAXA to explore the possibilities of, get this: mining the asteroid belt between Mars and Jupiter for precious metals and minerals of every sort!" Bobby paused his pacing broken by a fit of giggles. He regained his composure and continued, "This probe is the first step toward deep space mining. They're throwing a lot of money at this. It's not my concern how they choose to spend their money. It is my aim to build the most efficient radioisotope thermoelectric generator in the history of mankind to put in that probe."

"Estimate the end price they'll pay for your generator," Sean said.

Bobby didn't hesitate, "$600 million."

Randal jumped out of the stool and almost fell on the tiled floor, "You bastard!" he exclaimed. "You've been low-balling me for years!"

Still pacing, Bobby shrugged and said, "You never asked."

Randal took up his own wide eyed stare at the ceiling as he shook his head in disbelief.

Sean turned away from Randal and spoke to Bobby, "Alright. If my basic math is correct, we give you the ring for 30 percent less, that's 31.5 million. Two percent of 600 million is 12 million. 31.5 million plus 12 million is 43.5 million. That's 1.5 million less than the original offer of 45 million."

"Like I said; you never asked," Bobby said with no remorse.

Randal muttered curses, still staring at the ceiling.

"We're going to revise our numbers slightly," Sean said. "We'll take 25 percent off the $45 million, which comes to $33.75 million payable immediately."

"Are you nuts?" Randal blurted.

Sean continued as if Randal hadn't spoken, "And we'll take five percent of the final sale price. If it goes for $600 million, that'll be $30 million payable..."

"Deal." Bobby said.

Sean held up his hand, more for Randal's benefit, and continued, "Payable upon final sale. From that point forward," Sean turned away from Bobby and spoke directly to Randal, "we will forgo our sale price of future delivered products and take 20 percent of your final sale price."

"May I request certain products in the future?" asked Bobby.

"We'll see," Sean answered, still holding Randal's shocked stare.

Bobby sat down on a stool and turned his head from side to side, eyes rolling from empty point to point as he considered the offer. Randal and Sean continued to stare at one another, but Randal's look was slowly turning from shock to sly admiration.

Bobby finally sighed and stood up. "Business partners," he declared.

"Yes," Sean answered.

"Shall we draw up papers?" Bobby asked.

Sean gave a questioning look to Randal. Randal shook his head 'no'.

"That's not necessary," Sean said. "Thus far, this has been a relationship of professional trust. Let's keep it that way."

Bobby walked to Sean, trying to guess at eye contact, but staring just above Sean's left ear. Bobby held out his hand. Sean shook his hand and said, "We look forward to continuing our arrangement under these terms."

Bobby nodded in agreement.

"One more question," Sean said. "How will you ensure this product we've sold you today can't be traced back to Mr. McNeill and myself?"

"I have certain arrangements," Bobby said. He motioned to Randal and continued, "*Mr. McNeill* will fill you in."

Bobby turned away from Sean and began making his way back to the electric generator he'd been working on when they arrived. "Now if you'll excuse me," he said over his shoulder, "I'd like to get back to work. The 33.75 million will be transferred to the usual Grand Cayman account in less than an hour."

Randal turned on his heel and motioned for Sean to follow. "Nice doing business with you, Bobby. We'll be in touch."

Bobby Truman didn't answer. He was already busy turning dials on the spectrometer and running his fingers over Braille printouts.

1235 HOURS, 1 NOVEMBER 1998 – ALBEQUERQUE, NEW MEXICO

After confirming dinner plans with the buxom Miss Tessa Woodward, Randal McNeill and Sean Akkerman left the building and made their way to the SUV.

"Toss me the keys, Convert." It was Bradley Dorne again.

Josh underhanded the keys to Dorne. As soon as they got in, Dorne ripped out of the parking lot and headed back toward downtown Albuquerque.

"Don't worry about Bobby, Convert. He's solid with the operational security. Like I said, I've been working with him for years and he has ways of covering his tracks. Plus, remember me telling you how incompetent the US Government can be? They're not on to him, nor will they ever be. The only people Bobby has to worry about are the competing labs. They might get suspicious of his ability to acquire some of his materials, but he has ways of throwing them off. They all think he's a lot smarter than he is, and that he has more connections than he actually does. He's solid."

"I understand," Josh said.

"Now on to more pressing matters," Dorne said as he weaved through traffic on Interstate 40 west. "Well-freakin' done in there, Convert. You performed far beyond expectations. We need to see more of that. The near $40 million will more than cover your training costs, but you have to understand that Bobby is still mine. The money you or I make off him in the future will go toward my operations, got it?"

"Ok," Josh said. He had no idea what Dorne was talking about.

Dorne sensed Josh's confusion and said, "Don't worry about it. You'll catch on, and when you do remember that Bobby's still mine." He sighed and shrugged his shoulders, then said, "But I suppose what's mine is yours in the end." He looked over at Josh, who was still confused. "I'm not making this any better. Back to Bobby. You handled him perfectly, better than me in fact. You had concerns about the use of the plutonium, and you put those concerns to rest while benefiting your bargaining position. You didn't blindly trust me or Bobby. That can't be taught." Dorne stopped talking for a moment and tapped the steering wheel. "I just knew it. You're gonna do fine, Convert."

"Thanks," Josh said.

"I told you not to thank me," Dorne said. "You have any pressing questions about what you just did with Bobby?"

"I do," said Josh. "If our job is to tip the scales in favor of the United States, why didn't we try to get that plutonium ring back into the government's hands?"

"Too risky," Dorne said without hesitating. "My reason for being is to protect the Republic and the Constitution that regulates it. Sometimes that means protecting the government from itself. I simply don't trust the government to use a purloined ring of plutonium-239 properly. That ring would sit in a warehouse indefinitely while they conducted their investigation as to its origins. That ring could make its way to Pakistan or Saudi Arabia on some lame-ass State Department cultural exchange program. Plus, it would lead back to us. Can't have that."

Josh cocked his head to the side and asked, "So no one inside the US government knows we exist?"

Dorne chuckled a bit and answered, "So it's *we* now? No. No one in the US government knows we exist as we do. We're long forgotten, but that's another story for another Element to tell you. Sometimes someone or some agency will sniff our trail, but we've always managed to remain foggy if not outright invisible. That incident in Luxembourg, and the asshole who questioned you-- I've reported that, and we'll manage our way through it. Non-state actors or anomalies. Those are the conclusions they always reach."

"Who?" Josh asked. "Who reaches those conclusions?"

Dorne let out an exasperated sigh and said, "CIA, NKVD, FBI, KGB, OSS, US Marshals, ATF, INTERPOL, The Pinkertons, Secret Service, Mossad, the list goes on."

"OSS?" Josh asked. "As in Office of Strategic Services? Like from the 1940s?"

"Oh yes," Dorne answered. "We've been around a while." He merged onto Interstate 25 and took a second to rub his eyes. "Damn, I'm tired. I'm giving you way too much. You'll get to all that. Let's shut up for a minute."

Josh obliged as Dorne exited Interstate 25 and weaved his way through downtown Albuquerque. They pulled into the valet parking area of the fancy Hotel Andaluz. Dorne took two duffels and Josh gathered the third. Dorne checked into a top floor deluxe suite using yet another assumed name backed by drivers license and credit cards. Dorne declined bellhop service and had Josh help him get his bags upstairs. Dorne had Josh wait outside the suite while Dorne placed the duffels inside. Once finished, he had Josh escort him to the near empty hotel bar. Dorne ordered a whiskey neat and Josh ordered a light beer. They sat down in a booth near the back of the bar. Dorne finished his whiskey in one gulp and sank back into the booth. He rubbed his eyes and again, sighed deeply.

"Mm-hm," he muttered. "So that's done then."

"What now?" Josh asked.

Still rubbing his eyes, Dorne said, "I'll tell you what now. I'm going to drink two more whiskeys, go up and take a long shower, check my Grand Cayman account, make some secure transfers, take a nap, have a nice steak dinner with Miss Woodward, take her up to the room, we'll have our way with each other, and then I'm gonna sleep for about three days. Then it's back to work." He sighed again and swirled the empty glass as he eyed the bar.

Josh smiled at the idea, but realized he wasn't part of Dorne's plan in any way. "What now for me?"

Dorne took a thick letter sized envelope from inside his coat pocket. He placed it on the table and slid it to Josh.

"I'm going to give these instructions once," he began, "and only once. You will follow them to the letter or you're done. You won't ask any questions. When I'm finished talking, you'll get up and leave. Understand?"

Josh nodded.

"Good," he said. "In the envelope you'll find an address. You'll make your way to that address within 30 hours. You'll also find a key card inside the envelope. You will use the key card to enter the structure located at said address. You will await further instructions at your destination. Finally, you will find 1500 dollars. If you have a run in with the police or any authority and you are incarcerated, I will not help you. That happens only once, and you had your help in The Hague. You still have at least 750 more push-ups to do today. Keep working the racquetball. Do not fail, Convert."

Josh grabbed the envelope and slid it into his own coat pocket. He waited for a moment in case Dorne had anything else to say. Dorne simply got up from the table with his empty glass and walked to the bar. Josh took a deep breath and got to his feet. As he made his way to the hotel exit, he heard Dorne mutter a very satisfied 'Mm-hm' from the bar.

2040 HOURS, 2 NOVEMBER 1998 – BIAMONT, SOIGNIES, BELGIUM

Clovis Xavier Beebe tapped his West Point class of 1994 ring on the massive oak desk as he stared at his diploma, daydreaming of working on a Pentagon staff. Captain Beebe wasn't used to being at work this late in the evening, especially on a Monday night. Usually, he was hip deep in his den at home working on his Master's thesis concerning Napoleonic Era battlefields for Universite Libre de Bruxelles. Living in Europe at this point in his career had given him a unique opportunity to polish his education. One couldn't make General, after all, without a PhD nowadays. He'd have to write off the night of refining his thesis, and for good reason. When a young captain receives a call from the Army G2 instructing him to await a meeting with a 'senior representative', the young captain obliges. Beebe knew this meeting must be about the fiasco involving that insubordinate shit, Staff Sergeant Quinn. Although Beebe wasn't in the least bit at fault for the incident, he was Quinn's commanding officer. He'd spent the majority of the day formulating his explanation and compiling a historical file of Quinn's disobedience and defiance. Captain Clovis X. Beebe IV would be damned if a worthless Staff Sergeant would get in his way of fulfilling his family's tradition of cultivating flag officers. He tapped his ring on the desk and swung slightly in his chair, turning his stare to the West Point class of 1994 picture.

Three stiff knocks at the door shook him from his daydream. "Captain Beebe, sir?" It was Chief Smith. "Major Butler to see you."

Beebe pivoted in his chair and stood. His first thought was that a major was not an appropriate rank to represent the Army G2, but he was a 'senior representative' regardless of rank. Beebe planned to treat him accordingly. "Send him in," Beebe said sharply. He made his way around the desk, shot his cuffs and stood at attention as the door opened. When the man walked into the office, the first thing Captain Beebe noticed was his garish blue and yellow striped tie.

"Major Butler," the man said as he approached Beebe.

"Captain Beebe, sir," he answered as he held out his hand.

Butler ignored Beebe's outstretched hand and shouldered by him. He walked around the desk and surveyed the pictures and plaques on the wall around and behind the desk. Beebe didn't know what else to do but pivot on his heel and face the Major. This wasn't proper protocol. Major Butler took special interest in the West Point diploma on the wall just to the right of the desk. He examined it closely, then shook his head as he sighed and flopped down in Beebe's chair.

"Sit," Major Butler ordered. Beebe immediately obliged. This was most irregular and rude. Butler studied Beebe for a moment, then said, "I imagine it has been a long few days for you, Captain."

"It has," Beebe said. "It has. I assure you, Major Butler, I have filed the appropriate paperwork and have already drafted the necessary documents needed to prosecute Staff Sergeant Quinn to the fullest extent of the UCMJ."

Butler chuckled, "I'm sure you have. Tell me more about how you're not responsible."

Beebe completely missed Butler's disdain and began the dissertation he'd rehearsed all afternoon and evening. He pointed Major Butler to the file on his desk and urged him to review it. Butler simply pushed the file aside and leaned back in the chair, motioning for Beebe to continue. After only seven minutes, Beebe ran out of explanations and closed his argument with a powerful condemnation of Staff Sergeant Quinn and Quinn's supervisor Chief Smith. Beebe surprised even himself with the denunciation of Smith, but he could see Butler wasn't satisfied, so he extended the radius of blame on a whim.

"Phew!" Butler exclaimed. "Seems like those guys are in trouble!"

"They certainly are," Captain Beebe affirmed.

"Well that's all well and good, Captain," Butler said, "but I'm not at all interested in who is to blame. I know who is to blame." He paused and leaned forward. He nodded his head once at Beebe. "But like I said; I'm not interested. As you know, Staff Sergeant Quinn escaped INTERPOL custody." Major Butler suddenly stood from the chair and yelled at Beebe, "Why the fuck do you think I'm here? Pull your head out of your ass, Captain! Stand at attention when I speak to you!"

Beebe shot up out of his chair and locked in at attention.

"West Point, my ass," Butler sniffed as he sat back down. "Now you listen to me, and you listen good. I will ask you questions and you will give me exact and precise answers. Imagine I am God Almighty, because every night you pray to God Almighty that you'll make General. Although I cannot guarantee you will make General, I can guarantee you will not. Do you understand, Captain?"

"Yes, sir!" Beebe exclaimed.

"Good," Butler said as he pulled Joshua Quinn's file back in front of him and opened it. "Now. Take off your class ring."

Beebe turned his eyes to Butler, then shot them back straight. "Sir?"

"You heard me," Butler said as he perused the file. "Take off that class ring and lay it on the desk in front of me. At no point in this conversation do I wish to see the light reflected off that likely fake diamond in the center of that thing."

Beebe hesitated.

"Do it!" Butler snapped.

Beebe immediately raised his right hand, took the ring off with his left and laid it on the desk in front of Butler. He immediately snapped back to attention, although his eyes were still on the ring.

"Hey!" Butler exclaimed, "is that how they teach the position of attention at West Point?"

Beebe eyes left the ring and went forward.

"Now," Butler said, "tell me everything you know about Staff Sergeant Quinn."

Beebe recited when Joshua Quinn arrived at his unit, Quinn's duty description, the various missions he'd conducted, his date of rank, his re-enlistment date, his DEROS date and his ETS date.

Butler rolled his eyes and said, "Tell me about his personal life. Have you been to his apartment? Who are his friends? What does he do on leave? Has he exhibited any indicators of espionage? Has he exhibited any indicators of subversion or sabotage? Give me something here, Captain."

Beebe searched his mental index for answers to any of the questions Major Butler had asked. All he could do was indicate that the file contained Staff Sergeant Quinn's local address.

Butler shook his head and rubbed his eyes. He sighed and ordered Captain Beebe to the position of parade rest. "Listen, Beebe," he said. "You have to give me something. Try to relax. Your ass is on the line here." Butler chuckled a bit at his own comment, then continued, "What do you think about him?"

"Sir?"

"Goddam it," Butler said, "Just tell me what *you* think about this kid."

Beebe was puzzled. He wasn't used to giving his opinion to a senior officer, let alone while he was in the midst of an ass chewing. Beebe's mind paused for a moment, and he realized he'd never once had an ass chewing since his sophomore year at West Point.

"Captain," Major Butler was brushing a fingertip with the tip of his thumb.

"Yes sir," Beebe answered, "what I think of Staff Sergeant Quinn. Yes sir. I think Quinn is a trouble maker. Very little discipline, as you can see from his file. He doesn't belong in military intelligence. He belongs back where he came from--in the infantry."

"Does he?" Butler asked, still brushing his fingernails.

"Yes sir," Beebe said.

"Interesting," Butler said, shaking his head. "What was the most personal conversation you ever had with him?"

"Personal?" Beebe though for a moment. "I suppose it was when I first took command and gave him his first counseling as company commander. I asked him what he planned on doing with his career. He didn't give me an exact answer beyond he preferred to make the military a profession. I asked him what his goals were. Again, he gave no direct answer. I asked him if any member of his family ever served. He told me his grandfather served, but I can't recall his grandfather's name."

"Of course not," Butler said. "Do you have a written file of the counseling with notes?" Beebe sheepishly nodded that he did not. "Again, of course not," Butler sighed. "You're on thin ice here, Captain. I'm waiting for something."

"Yes, sir," Beebe searched for something, anything. He'd never been to Quinn's apartment. He wouldn't have been caught dead in that part of Biamont. Who are his friends? Beebe had no idea. What does he do on leave? That's it! "Sir, Major Butler. Staff Sergeant Quinn filed for extended leave three times. Each for two weeks at a time. The destination of each leave location was Columbus, Georgia. When asked what his plans were in Columbus, he said he was simply going home to see his family. I thought this was odd since his home of record is listed as San Marcos, Texas." Beebe stopped right there, hoping it was enough.

"I see," Butler said. "Captain, I could have found that in his file, but I suppose you've saved me some reading time." He sighed, put his feet up on the desk and folded his hands behind his head as a paperweight fell off the desk and landed with a thud. Butler stayed in this position for a few moments in silence, then said, "Yes. That's enough."

"Thank you, sir," Beebe said.

"Oh you're not off the hook yet, Captain," Butler said without moving his feet off the desk. "What about this Bradley Dorne character?"

Beebe cocked his head to the side and said carefully, "Sir, my commander in Brussels instructed me that portion of this incident is sealed and I'm not to speak of it."

Butler sighed deeply and pivoted his feet off the desk, knocking over another one of Beebe's ostentatious mementos. He stood and leaned on his fists over the desk. "Captain," he breathed, "who in the fuck do you think gave your commander those instructions? Good God," he said as he shook his head and stared at Beebe, "you are the dumbest and sorriest excuse for an officer I've ever encountered."

Beebe's eyes were wide. He'd never in his life been spoken to in this manner. All he could muster was a weak "Sir?"

Butler brought his hands to his forehead and rubbed. "Beebe," he began, "Tell me what you know about Bradley Dorne."

Beebe wasn't taking chances at this point. He knew he was one foolish comment away from a ruined career. He spoke about Dorne for about two minutes, relating the events of 24 October 1998. Within those two minutes Beebe told Butler everything he knew about Dorne, which according to Butler's reactions, was nothing.

Butler stopped rubbing his forehead and took two casual steps to his right. He stopped at the wall and looked up at the West Point class of 1996 group photograph. He studied the photo in silence for what seemed to Beebe like an eternity. "Captain," Butler declared.

"Yes sir," Beebe answered. A trickle of sweat ran down his cheek.

"Are you on my side?"

"Sir?"

Butler continued to study the class photo. "Are you on my side? Can you help me in this matter and matters that present themselves in the future? Because at this point, without me you are simply a ladder-climbing flunky future Colonel? Because I will not suffer flunky Colonel. If you're on my side, you'll make General Officer, Captain."

"I'm on your side," Beebe said immediately.

"Excuse me?"

Beebe shook his head and another bead of sweat rolled down the back of his ear. He corrected himself and said enthusiastically, "I'm on your side, sir!"

"Good answer," Butler said. He turned from the photo and strode directly toward Beebe as if he meant to inflict violence. Beebe flinched when Butler reached him and stood chest to chest. Butler leaned in to Beebe's sweaty ear and whispered, "Tonight is your lucky night, Captain Beebe. Your career isn't the only thing I am able bring to an end, you know. It is true you're worthless. It is true you're an idiot. You may be lying when you say you're on my side. But this," Butler brought his left fist down on Beebe's right collar. Beebe squealed and his knees buckled from the pain of the U.S. pin digging into his collarbone. "This!" Butler said in a loud whisper, "I'll respect this for now. The next time you see me, General or not, you show me some respect."

"Yes sir," Beebe answered with a pathetic whimper.

Butler put his hand on Beebe's chest and pushed him down into the chair. He pivoted back to the desk and collected Beebe's class ring. He leaned to the right and tossed the ring into the waste basket. He chuckled as he turned and walked out of Beebe's office. "Until next time, Captain."

Captain Clovis X. Beebe remained in the chair for at least twenty minutes. He finally gathered himself and sat up, rubbing his right collar bone. He leaned forward until he was out of the chair and on all fours. He crawled to the waste basket and fished out his class ring. He sat back on the floor with his back against the front of his massive oak desk. He wiped a tear from his cheek and slid the ring back on his finger.

0045 HOURS, 3 NOVEMBER 1998 – TBILISI, GEORGIA

Noah Goldstein staggered out of the local Georgian bar and into the cool evening with just 15 minutes to spare. He was far drunker than usual, but this was a celebration. He'd used the bearer bonds to pay out his assets and to 'reimburse' certain high level politicians and military officers for the missing plutonium. In the end, it had cost him a lot less than he'd planned. When all was said and done, he had pocketed 50 million dollars in this deal. So this was a celebration. He was done with showing up to the office, even with 27 more days of work before retirement.

"Screw them," he slurred as he veered into a wall.

If they chose, they could go ahead and take away his retirement for not showing up to work. But they wouldn't. Once in 1974, he didn't show up to his station in Berlin for 45 days. Even when they found out he had been on a sex crazed romp in Majorca with a the juicy new Berlin station intern, they didn't do crap. And they wouldn't do crap now.

He staggered into another wall and burped. A bit of vomit came up, but he swallowed it back down. No time to get sick now, he thought. Noah brought his wrist to his face and studied his watch. It seemed he only had about 10 more minutes to get back to his home. He belched again, straightened his coat and continued down the sidewalk toward his flat. Tonight was the night, he just knew it. His secretary Mandy had promised, *promised* this time that she'd show up at his flat at one in the morning. Sure, he'd passively threatened her with a promotion denial if she didn't show up, but all is fair. Noah chuckled. He'd grabbed her ass or her tits as she passed him in the office plenty of times. She always jumped when he did that, but he knew what it meant. All these tarts are the same; they need a little warming up. A little encouragement. She'd told him she'd show up before, but she hadn't yet. But this time her job may be on the line. She'll be there.

Noah was starting to get excited. Only a couple more blocks to his apartment and about five minutes to get there. He belched, but this time he had to lean over and vomit.

"Ahhhhh!" he groaned.

It always cleared everything a bit to throw up. He shook his head and checked his watch. Four minutes. She'd probably be there waiting when he arrived. He scratched his crotch and began walking again.

He barely noticed the three young men in black leather jackets round the next corner. He was too busy flexing his hands preparing them for Mandy's body as they walked directly toward him. He bumped the first young man and muttered, 'excuse me' in Russian.

The young man stopped and grabbed Noah by the lapel.

"Russian?!" The kid said in Georgian, "what the hell country you think you're in, old faggot?" He grabbed Noah's other lapel and shoved him against the wall.

The moment Noah's back and head slammed against the wall he heard another voice say, "Careful, Djokia! The American man said to make it look like a mugging--"

Noah felt a hard punch hit him just below the ribs. Then another. Then another. Then another. The young man backed away and Noah hit the ground, clutching his gut. He felt another sharp punch in his kidneys. Then another. Then another. He barely felt his wallet come out of his back pocket and his shoes come off his feet. He then heard the sound of feet slapping the pavement running away.

Noah tried to get up, but his head was too light. He noticed the ground seemed very, very cold. His gut and his lower back ached like never before. He brought his hand to his gut just under the ribs to rub the area, but his hand just slid and he heard a sloshing sound. Had he been stabbed? Surely not. He couldn't feel a thing now. The cold was going away and now he felt a warmth growing within his chest. He smiled and hoped Mandy would wait as he slipped away.

0645 HOURS, 10 NOVEMBER 1998 – YORK COUNTY, PENNSYLVANIA

He'd driven straight through the night, yet he was going to be at least 15 minutes early. He congratulated himself on an all-around job well done. Visiting Conrad Schreiber was tradition after a successful mission. Point of fact, it was tradition to visit him even after unsuccessful missions, but after unsuccessful missions Conrad Schreiber was Element 1. Fortunately, he visited Conrad Schreiber about 9 out of 10 times.

He turned off of Route 425 onto a dirt road and drove a few hundred meters to a large farm house surrounded by silos and barns. The sun was starting to creep up, slightly thawing the early autumn frost on the house and the silos. He smiled as he approached the old structure. Being here for only a few hours was always a welcome respite from what his chaotic and messy life had become. He took a deep breath and angled around the driveway in front of the house. He put the car in park, shut it off and opened the door. He grabbed the sack of fast food breakfast and made his way toward the front porch.

The sound of an ax hitting wood behind the house was unmistakable. He smiled and shook his head as he changed his direction from the front door and headed around back. When he rounded the corner, he saw Conrad wearing work boots, jeans and a tank top, chopping wood with a double headed ax.

"For God's sake, Conrad," he said as he walked toward him, "it's only 31 degrees out here. Put on some clothes, old man."

Conrad buried the ax in a small log, splitting it into pieces. "Old man? Just once, I'd like to see you do some real work. Real work keeps a man young, son."

Element 65 turned up his collar against the chill and said, "Alright, alright. At least come inside and have breakfast with me."

Conrad pulled the ax free and then swung it gain, burying it in the chopping stump. "So it's Conrad this time. That's always a good sign. Come on in and warm yourself up, boy. I've had a fire going since four this morning."

Once inside, Conrad and Element 65 seated themselves in the massive den, ate their sausage and egg sandwiches and made small talk about the weather and the upcoming deer season. After they finished their breakfast, they sat and watched the fire for a few minutes. Conrad broke the silence and said, "So it's been a while."

"Yeah," said Element 65, still mesmerized by the flames.

"So who were you most of the time since I last saw you?" asked Conrad.

Element 65 broke his stare from the fire and leaned back, rubbing his face with his palms, trying to remember. "Ah, let's see. Bradley Dorne, I think."

"Dorne," Conrad said. "Decent Irish name. Let's use that name this time."

"Fine with me," said Dorne.

"Let's talk, then," said Conrad. "I've heard the rough points surrounding your latest mission. A success; yes, but I believe we have a few things to discuss. Don't sugar coat it. What do I need to know?"

"I got the plutonium," Dorne said, "but I have to believe the whole thing was a dangle. I caught it early enough, but I couldn't let it go. I called in way more support than usual, but I think it was worth it."

"I concur the plutonium ring was a set-up. What is your level of compromise?" asked Conrad.

"Manageable," Dorne replied.

"Explain," Conrad said. He was sounding more and more like Element 1.

Dorne sighed and outlined how he'd have to permanently expunge three identities he'd had running for years that could be tied to the operation, including Bradley Dorne. He'd have to lay off the Russian Mafia and Europe for at least a couple of years, and he wouldn't be able to co-opt the military for at least 12 months. That would limit his operations considerably, but he had a few leads in southwest Asia and the Caucuses he'd be able to run down.

When Dorne finished Conrad asked, "Was this plutonium ring an existential threat to this country?"

"Not by itself," Dorne replied. "But what is, there days?" He sighed and looked back at the fire, "Beside the obvious."

Conrad nodded and asked, "Were any Seraphs, Deacons or fellow

Ministers compromised?"

"No," Dorne said. "The Seraphs and Deacons were purely support. I called in light air support from a Deacon I've used in the past, but I followed up with her and she's safe in Portugal with her air asset. One Seraph provided UAV support from across the ocean, and the craft was destroyed. According to him, the UAV was damaged beyond tracing and the auto- destruct took care of any compromising technologies."

"I see," said Conrad. "These dangles and set-ups are becoming a trend. This is the third in two years. We're sure it isn't CIA, FBI, DoD or NSA. We're deeply penetrated in those organizations, as you know. We must be dealing with something new."

"My thoughts exactly," Dorne said, nodding and staring into the fire. "The guys that came after me were plainly trained by US military at some point, albeit, not very well. I know for a fact the one who took the new Convert was American."

"Ah yes," Conrad said, "the new Convert. It's obvious this is what you really want to talk about this morning. I was beginning to believe you'd never find yours."

"I didn't just find my understudy Minister. Conrad, he's the one," Dorne said.

"Really?" asked Conrad. "Considering all we've discussed over the years? You believe you've found the one?"

"He's not like us," Dorne answered. "We're not sufficiently objective. We all share the same traits concerning justice and meeting ends, but this kid takes it to a whole other level. I've never seen, heard or read about anything like his condition. It's like ours, but much more controlled and severe. If he makes it through his training and indoctrination, he'll give us our answer."

Conrad Schreiber took a deep breath, then let it out slowly. "Our answer," he said as he exhaled. "The answer to the question we can't clearly formulate, the answer you and I know is imperative, yet the answer no one wants. Have you discussed this with him at all? Tell me you weren't that foolish."

"I slipped a couple of times," Dorne said. "I told him there is a storm coming, and that he's the one for whom I'd been waiting, but those phrases could mean anything to him in his current state."

"What are his odds of becoming an Element?" asked Conrad.

"Same as any of us," answered Dorne. "He started his training and indoctrination a week ago and so far he looks like the rest of us did at this point in the training. If there's an accident, then this whole thing just isn't meant to be. If he drops out or is deemed unsuitable by the Elders, Deacons or Ministers, then we'll have to keep looking for our answer."

They both sat in silence for a few minutes staring at the fire, not contemplating the answer, but pondering the resolution if the answer were ever to be brought to light. Dorne broke his stare to check his watch.

"I have a flight out of Dulles at 1500, Conrad. I have to pick up a new identity from the Seraphs in DC on the way out. I'm going to have to get on the road."

Conrad got up out of his chair and shook Dorne's hand. "Thank you for stopping by. Where are you heading?"

"Azerbaijan via Turkey," said Dorne. "A fellow Minister has reached out, and I have nothing better to do now that Europe's shut down for me."

As they walked down the hall toward the front door, Conrad assured Dorne that he and the other Elders would reach out to a few Deacons, Seraphs and Ministers to look into the trending set-ups and dangles. They'd also make sure Dorne's tracks were sufficiently covered from his most recent operation. "I'll also be mentoring your new Convert as I mentored you way back when," he added. "But we have to let him make up his own mind."

"Don't worry," Dorne shut the car door and rolled down the window, "you won't have any problems with this kid like you did with me. Until next time, Conrad."

Dorne sped out of driveway and headed south toward Maryland.

"That remains to be seen," Conrad muttered staring at Dorne racing south. Shaking his head and sighing, the old man went around to the rear of the cabin and picked up his ax again.

EPILOGUE

Austin American Times-Herald
Dateline: November 11, 1998
Section D, Page 4
Obituaries

QUINN, Joshua Dante, Born March 21, 1970 in Virginia Beach, Virginia. Died October 29, 1998 in Amsterdam, The Netherlands. Preceded in death by his mother, Jenette Anne Quinn, nee Sabol. Living relatives: Sister, Victoria Anne Quinn. Joshua was honorably serving his country as a Staff Sergeant in the US Army at the time of his death. He was a graduate of Brownwood High School and attended Southwest Texas State University in San Marcos where he graduated with a Bachelor of Arts in Political Science in 1992. At Southwest Texas State, Joshua lettered four years in both football and track and field. Though he will be missed, his spirit and patriotism will live on and continue to be felt by those he left behind. Burial by cremation. No services scheduled.

ABOUT THE AUTHOR

AJ Todd grew up in Texas and the Southwest United States. Todd earned a Bachelor of Arts degree in English Literature and Philosophy from Texas Tech University. Todd continues to heed the call of duty and serves as a career military man with multiple combat tours. He has lived, worked and traveled throughout Europe, the Middle East, Asia and South America. Todd is married to the love of his life, Michelle, and they share two wonderful children who astound them daily. The family shares their home in Texas with a menagerie of cats and dogs: Hazel, Dash, Thor, Clyde, Pickle and Snoop. AJ Todd writes military, thriller, speculative, dystopian, action, and time travel short stories, short novels, and novels.

Made in the USA
Middletown, DE
19 May 2016